YOU MAKE ME FEEL SO DEAD

Be the King of Rock & Roll's bodyguard? Eddie Gianelli is about to face his toughest challenge yet

It's 1964, and Elvis Presley is heading to Vegas for the opening of his latest film, *Viva Las Vegas*. When his manager contacts Frank Sinatra to request his help in safeguarding Elvis while he's in Vegas, Frank calls on Eddie as being just the man for the job. Unfortunately Eddie must also find out who put his friend, Vegas PI Danny Bardini, in hospital – and why. Eddie will need to call on his old friends, the Rat Pack, for help if he is to rise to the challenge.

* *available from Severn House*

YOU MAKE ME FEEL SO DEAD

A 'Rat Pack' Mystery

Robert J. Randisi

Severn House Large Print
London & New York

This first large print edition published 2015
in Great Britain and the USA by
SEVERN HOUSE PUBLISHERS LTD of
19 Cedar Road, Sutton, Surrey, England, SM2 5DA.
First world regular print edition published 2013 by
Severn House Publishers Ltd., London and New York.

British Library Cataloguing in Publication Data

Randisi, Robert J. author.
  You make me feel so dead.
  1. Presley, Elvis, 1935-1977--Fiction. 2. Rat Pack
  (Entertainers)--Fiction. 3. Gianelli, Eddie (Fictitious
  character)--Fiction. 4. Las Vegas (Nev.)--Fiction.
  5. Detective and mystery stories. 6. Large type books.
  I. Title
  813.6-dc23

  ISBN-13: 9780727897466

Severn House Publishers support the Forest Stewardship Council™
[FSC™], the leading international forest certification organisation. All
our titles that are printed on FSC certified paper carry the FSC logo.

Printed and bound in Great Britain by
T J International, Padstow, Cornwall.

'You Make Me Feel So Young'

Music by Josef Myrow,
lyrics by Mack Gordon 1946

To Marthayn, you make me feel so loved

PROLOGUE

Spring 2007

Elvis was in the building.

In *my* building.

No, I'm serious.

My first clue was the rhinestones on the floor. Of the elevator, that is. I felt them under my feet when I got in, then looked down at them. Three or four, lying on the metal floor. Not real, of course. They couldn't be.

I didn't think anything about them until a few days later. I was in the lobby again, waiting to take the elevator up to my floor. When the doors opened a young guy stepped out, with slicked-back black hair and long sideburns.

He looked a heck of a lot like Elvis Presley.

Of course, he was most likely an Elvis impersonator. Vegas was full of shows featuring legend impersonators: Dolly Parton, Cher, Joan Rivers, Frank and Dino and, of course, Elvis. You could even hear their voices over the loudspeakers at the airport.

He passed me as I got in the elevator, then

turned, reached out and stopped the doors from closing.

'Excuse me, sir?'

'Yes?'

'Are you – you're Eddie Gianelli, aren't you? Eddie G.?'

'That's right,' I said. 'Do I know you?'

'No, sir,' he said, 'but I've heard of you. You knew them.'

'Them?' I asked. 'Who's them?'

'All of them,' he said. 'Frank, Dino, Sammy ... you knew them.'

'I did,' I said. 'They were my friends.'

'That is so cool,' he said. 'Do you mind if I ask you—'

'This is not really a good time.' I was in a hurry to get to my apartment. I'd gone for a walk, but as is the way with octogenarian bladders, mine was barking.

'Oh, I'm sorry,' he said. 'Look, my name's Roger Bennett. I'm an Elvis impersonator.'

'Where?'

'Excuse me?'

'What show?'

'Oh, MGM Grand.'

'Good place to work.'

'Yes, it is. Look, could I talk to you some time? Have a drink? Maybe I can buy you lunch?'

'I eat lunch,' I said. 'Don't drink as much as I used to.'

'Could we do it tomorrow, maybe?' he asked,

10

anxiously. 'I'd like to talk to you about the way Vegas used to be. I – I think it would help me in my performance.'

'Well ... sure, why not?' I said. 'Meet me here in the lobby at noon.'

'Hey, that's great!' he said, happily. 'Thanks.'

'Sure.'

We stood there a minute and then I said, 'The doors?'

'Oh, sure,' he said, with a start. 'I just...'

'What?'

'Did you know him?' he asked. 'Did you know ... him, too?'

'Did I know who?'

He licked his lips, then said, 'Elvis.'

So that was it.

'Yeah,' I said, 'yeah, I knew Elvis.' I reached out and moved his hand from the doors. 'I'll tell you about it tomorrow.'

That night I made myself a small dinner. Eating was still a pleasure, but at my age I wasn't able to consume as much as I used to. I broiled a small steak and onions and potatoes, and prepared a salad. Afterward I sat in my armchair with a small glass of good bourbon. Roger wanted me to share some tales of old Vegas with him. Well, I wasn't averse to doing that. I may have occasionally forgotten things on a day-to-day basis, but my memories of the old days were still very vivid.

I stood up and carried the glass to the

window. My tenth floor window afforded me a good view of the Strip, which blazed with neon until dawn, when the sun came up and the lights went out. Sometimes, I actually stood there until it happened. Just as I didn't eat as much as I used to, I also didn't sleep as much. There were times I needed more than a little bourbon just so I could catch a couple of hours.

But on this night I decided to watch the lights, and bring back what I was going to tell Roger the next day, at lunch...

ONE

Las Vegas

May 1964

It was my first day off in weeks. The Sands had had a progression of whales – big time gamblers – come in, and Jack Entratter had wanted me around to help cater to their needs. Which meant that anything other casino employees couldn't get for them, I probably could. Sometimes I regretted the fact that everyone thought Eddie G. had Vegas wired.

I was eating a meager breakfast of toast and coffee, wondering what to do with my day, when my doorbell rang. I don't have a lot of people who drop by, so traditionally, that usually signaled bad news. Why should today be any different?

Dressed casually in T-shirt and jeans – since it *was* my day off – I went to the door and opened it, was shocked to see my boss, Jack Entratter, standing there.

'Quick,' he said, 'inside.'

13

'Wha—' I started, as he pushed past me.

'Close the door!'

I closed the door, turned to face him. He was dressed as well as usual – his expertly tailored suit still seeming to burst at the seams as it tried to contain his shoulders – but his manner was more harried than I'd seen in some time.

'Jack,' I asked, 'what's wrong? I can count on the fingers of one hand the times you've been ... No wait, you've never been to my house.'

'I know,' he said, looking around. 'It's kind of small, ain't it?'

'I like it,' I answered, defensively.

'No, no,' Entratter said, 'it's nice. Look, you know how I hate to bother you on your day off.'

I didn't know that at all, but I let it go.

'You want some coffee?' I asked.

'Sure.'

'Come into the kitchen.'

I led him into my – admittedly – small kitchen and poured him a cup. He sat at my table, dwarfing it. I sat across from him with a fresh cup for myself.

'What's on your mind?' I asked.

'Have you heard anything about Elvis comin' to town?' he asked.

'What?'

'Elvis,' he said, 'Presley. Ever heard of him?'

I stared at him. That was what he came to my house to discuss? Elvis?

'Well?'

'I heard some talk,' I said.

'From where?'

I shrugged. 'Sources.'

'And you didn't tell me?'

'Well,' I said, 'I didn't hear that he was comin' here to the Sands. And if he *is* comin' to the Sands, I figured you'd know.'

'He's comin',' Jack said, 'and he ain't comin' to us.'

'So what's the problem?'

'I don't know what the problem is, but I do know there is one,' he said. 'And I didn't want anybody hearin' us talkin' about Elvis.'

'So that's it?' I asked. 'I can get back to my day off now?'

'No, that ain't it,' Entratter said. 'Don't be in such a goddamned hurry!'

'OK, OK,' I said. 'Just get to it. I've got to make up my mind to either do laundry, or go grocery shopping.'

'I don't think you're gonna want to do either of those things,' he said. 'Look, Frank wants to talk to you.'

'Why didn't he call me himself?'

'He called ahead,' Entratter said. 'He'll be here any minute. He wanted me to have you available.'

'Available for what?'

'To talk, at first,' Entratter said. 'After that, I don't know. I'll need you to tell me what's goin' on after you see him.'

'OK,' I said, 'so I'll see Frank. Wait, does he

15

want to talk to me about Elvis, too, or is this something separate?'

'No no, it's all got to do with that Presley kid.'

I knew that Frank wasn't crazy about the singer and his music, but I also knew when Elvis came back from serving in Germany and appeared on Frank's show that the chairman had a change of heart. He started saying that Elvis wasn't 'a bad kid'.

'Let's get back to the Sands,' Entratter said. 'I'll find out if he's in his suite. And don't mention Elvis where anybody can hear us!'

'OK, I won't,' I said. Geez. I knew Elvis was the King, but what did Jack expect, a stampede at the mere mention of his name?

I went into my bedroom for my shoes. Veronica had rolled over in bed, causing the sheet to slip down so that her high, firm, showgirl tits were revealed. Her long black hair was fanned out on the pillow beneath her head. After we'd made love the night before she had threatened me by telling me, 'I am not a breakfast girl, so don't wake me up. Just go and make yourself some breakfast.' Which I had done. So I assumed she had slept through Jack's visit, and hadn't heard a thing about Elvis Presley.

Since I was off the clock I decided to stay casual and not wear a suit. I did, however, decide to take a windbreaker with me, because what people who don't live in the desert don't know is that it does get cold once the sun goes down.

I had been trying not to stare at Veronica, because the sheet was slipping further and further down. Her dark nipples had impressed me the night before, standing out as they did when distended, but now they were soft. Nevertheless, I was still fascinated, and staring at her might have delayed my departure.

I walked to the bed, leaned over and kissed her on both nipples. They immediately reacted, and she moaned.

'Are you wakin' me up for breakfast?' she demanded sleepily.

'Wouldn't think of it,' I said. 'Just sayin' good-bye.'

'Catch you down the road, Eddie G.,' she said, and turned over.

That was what I liked about Veronica. No sentiment.

TWO

Frank was in his suite, having only just arrived. But he wanted me to come right up.

Entratter had taken a limo to my house, so he rode back in it while I drove my Caddy. So much for my day off.

'You're off the clock,' Entratter reminded me, walking me to the elevator. 'I'll get somebody to cover your pit.'

'How do we even know I'll need to be replaced?' I asked. 'We don't know what Frank needs.'

'Whatever it is,' Entratter said, 'you're gonna give it to him.'

'OK, but we still don't know that I can't go right back to work.'

'Come on, Eddie,' he said, as the elevator opened. 'We been through this too many times before. We both know what's gonna happen.'

I stepped into the elevator and said, 'Yeah, we do.' The door closed.

Frank answered the door himself. That pretty much meant he'd left George Jacobs, his much valued valet, back at home, and was on his own.

'Hey, pally,' Frank said. 'Glad you could make it on short notice.'

'Jack dragged me out of my house and told me you wanted to see me,' I said. 'Something about Elvis?'

'That's right.'

'I thought you hated him.'

'Ah, he's not such a bad kid,' Frank said, as I'd expected. 'We got along when he did my special. But do you know who I really got along with?'

'Who?'

'The Colonel.'

'What Colonel?'

'Colonel Parker,' Frank said, 'Elvis' manager. You want a drink?'

'It's a little early.'

Frank went around the bar. He was looking thin. The events of 1963 – JFK's assassination, and the kidnapping of Frank Jr – had taken a lot out of him. I had seen him a few times since then, and it seemed to me he'd lost the capacity for joy. And he'd become overly protective of all his kids.

'How about something soft?' he asked.

'I'll have a Coke.'

I walked to the bar and sat on a stool. Frank had a blue, short-sleeved shirt on with a wide, white collar and grey slacks.

'Are you performing anywhere in town?' I

19

asked, as he set a glass of Coke in front of me.

'No,' Frank said. 'I think I'll catch Darin's act while I'm here, but I'm really in Vegas to do a favor for a friend.'

'Elvis?'

'I said he wasn't a bad kid,' Frank said. 'I didn't say we were friends. No, I'm talking about Colonel Parker.'

'OK,' I said, 'you're doing a favor for Parker. Where do I come in?'

'Right there,' Frank said, pouring himself a Coke, which surprised me. 'You see, the Colonel *is* in charge of every aspect of Elvis' life, but lately Elvis has been rebelling. He doesn't want to do the movies that the Colonel and the studio have picked out for him, any-more. He wants more serious parts.'

'Well, I saw him in *Jailhouse Rock* and *Love Me Tender*. Also *Flaming Star*. I didn't think he was too bad.'

'Yeah, well, those movies didn't make the money the other stuff did. The fans want to see Elvis sing and be surrounded by pretty girls.'

'That's not too hard to understand.'

'Well, he's coming to town to promote *Viva Las Vegas* with Ann-Margret.'

'Tough work.'

'The problem is, he's bringing the Memphis Mafia with him,' Frank said.

'What's that? Like his Summit? Or a biker gang?'

Frank laughed derisively and said, 'Not even

close. They're a bunch of no-talent losers who enable all of his bad habits.'

'Like what?'

'Like pills.'

'Elvis has a habit?'

'He's well on his way to having a habit, according to the Colonel,' Frank said. 'He's also looking for a new religion.'

'New religion?'

'He used to sing in the choir when he was a kid,' Frank said, 'but since the death of his mother he's having second thoughts about God.'

'Sounds like he's pretty mixed up.'

'He is,' Frank said, 'and the Colonel is afraid he's going to get himself in trouble while he's here.'

Uh-oh. I sensed a babysitting job coming.

'Frank—'

'Now, don't say anything,' Frank said. 'I know you're about to turn this gig down.'

'Gig? Are you offering to pay me?'

'Hell, no,' Frank said. 'We're pals. But the Colonel, he wants to meet you, and if you take the job, he'll pay you.'

'Wait a minute,' I said. 'Colonel Parker is here?'

'Well, not in the hotel,' Frank said. 'In fact, he's not even in Las Vegas. He rented a house out by Lake Mead.'

'So where does he want to meet me?'

'Out there,' Frank said. 'He doesn't want

Elvis to find out he's here. They've been having enough trouble lately without the kid thinking the Colonel is spying on him.'

'So he wants to hire me to do the spying?'

'As far as Elvis knows, you'll be showing him around town,' Frank said, 'because you and I are friends.'

'It's still a babysitting job, Frank.'

'Don't you want to meet the King, Eddie?' Frank asked.

'Come on, Frank,' I said, 'you know you're the King.'

'Don't kiss my ass, Eddie,' Frank said, but he was amused.

THREE

The last time I'd been out to Lake Mead I'd stayed in a cabin with Marilyn Monroe. This time, I didn't find a cabin when I got there, but an impressive two-story house with a rustic deck surrounding it. On the deck stood a man wearing a pale grey suit and a matching cowboy hat.

Colonel Tom Parker was in his mid-fifties, not an overly tall man, with a slight paunch and double chin. For years he claimed to have been born in the US, but in fact he was born Andreas Cornelis van Kuijk in Breda, Netherlands. He did not, however, speak with any sort of accent.

I parked, got out of the Caddy and walked to the foot of the steps.

'Mr Gianelli?' he asked, looking down at me.

'That's right.'

'Come on up, then,' he said. 'Thank you very much for coming.'

I went up the steps to join him on the deck. He was holding a glass of amber liquid.

'Would you like a drink?'

It had been a long ride from Vegas and I was a bit dry.

'Sure,' I said. 'I'll have what you're having.'

'Ice tea,' he said. 'I'll be right back.'

I was surprised when he came back with the drink himself. I'd expected to find him ensconced in such a house with lots of domestic help.

'There you go,' he said, handing me the sweating glass. 'Have a seat.'

There was a solid wooden table with matching chairs on the deck. I sat, and he sat across from me. There was a slight breeze since we were near the lake, and it stirred the ends of the western string tie he was wearing.

'I appreciate you coming out to see me,' he said.

'Well,' I said, 'Frank asked me to do it, as a favor.'

'I also appreciate that,' he said. 'Frank's a good friend.'

'He is that.'

'Did he tell you why I wanted to see you?'

'Frank said he'd leave that to you.'

'Good, good,' Parker said. 'I don't want this to come out wrong, and it might ... uh, I mean, coming from someone other than me.'

'I'm all ears,' I said, sipping the tea.

'There are a lot of people who think I control Elvis Presley,' Parker said. 'They couldn't be more wrong. Elvis controls Elvis. He makes his own decisions.'

'Based on your advice.'

He hesitated, then said, 'Yes. He takes financial advice from me. He takes artistic advice from no one. He picks the songs he's going to record, and the venues he's going to play.'

'I feel a "but" coming.'

'But ... he has friends, hangers-on, who are...' He was at a loss for words.

'Leading him astray?'

'Let's say that.'

'OK,' I agreed, 'let's.'

'He's coming to town to promote *Viva Las Vegas*, and he's bringing them with him. I'd like to make sure he doesn't take a wrong turn.'

'Colonel Parker,' I said, 'I'm just a guy from Brooklyn. I'm gonna need you to talk a little plainer to me.'

He leaned forward and looked at me earnestly. I had heard that Parker always had the air of a showman, a carnival barker, but now he appeared to be deadly serious.

'The boy is on the verge of making some disastrous choices,' he said, 'involving religion, business, and maybe ... drugs.'

'What kind of drugs?' I asked.

'I can't give you the names, but believe me, they're the bad kind.'

'Not prescription, then?'

'Some, maybe, but not all,' Parker said.

'And what about religion?'

Parker sat back, squinted at me.

'Since his mother died he's been looking for

... something. Comfort, I suppose. I'm afraid he might end up involved with some kind of cult, maybe Hare Krishnas, or worse.'

I sat back, placed my half finished ice tea on the table.

'What do you want me to do, Colonel?'

'Frank tells me you're the Man in Las Vegas,' Parker said. 'You got this town wired. If anybody can keep Elvis out of trouble, it's you.'

'I can't babysit him, if that's what you want, Colonel.'

'I don't want you to babysit him, Mr Gianelli,' Parker said. 'I want you to be his friend.'

FOUR

Elvis Presley's friend?

That was quite a thought. True, I'd never expected to become friends with Frank Sinatra, Dean Martin and Sammy Davis, Jr. Then again, working at the Sands I'd become friendly with other celebrities like Joey Bishop, Richard Conte, Nat King Cole – actors, singers, other kinds of performers.

But Elvis? The young King of Rock 'n Roll?

There was a mystique about Elvis, probably fostered by Colonel Tom Parker. But right now Parker sounded more like a worried parent. Could it be he looked on Elvis as a son, rather than a commodity to be managed?

'I think you want me to give Elvis a little more than friendship, Colonel.'

'Seems to me you're about ten or twelve years older than Elvis, Mr Gianelli.'

'Just call me Eddie, Colonel,' I said, 'and yes, about that.'

'Well, you'd be a better friend – even a big brother type – to him than that bunch he's running with.'

27

'The Memphis Mafia?'

Parker closed his eyes. 'I hate that name. The press gave it to them. I'm talking about Red and Sonny West, Marty Lacker, Larnar Fike. And a few others. They're all coming with him. He gives them anything they want. He gives them things they don't want, like cars, televisions. They don't even have to ask.'

'He's generous,' I said. 'Everybody knows that. He gave Sammy Davis an expensive belt buckle.'

'That's true,' Parker said, 'but Sammy Davis isn't leading him down the garden path. Sammy Davis isn't supplying him with pills to get up, and pills to get down.'

'Speed?' I asked.

'Among other things.'

Suddenly, he was able to name something.

'Look,' Parker said, 'he's coming to town to promote the film. I don't want him getting his name in the papers for anything ... bad.'

'I've got a question.'

'What?'

'Is Ann-Margret also coming to town?'

'She is.'

'She and Elvis were supposed to have been lovers while they were filming the movie,' I said. 'Was that true?'

Parker hesitated, then said, 'Yes.'

'Are they still lovers?'

'They haven't seen each other for some time, but since they'll be in town together, and they are both ... volatile people ... I expect they'll pick up where they left off.'

'You don't expect me to keep him away from her, do you?'

'Of course not,' Parker said. 'She's a sweet kid. I'd rather Elvis spend time with her than with his buddies.'

'If I agree to do this,' I said, 'what are you going to tell Elvis about me?'

'That you're friends with Frank, and Frank wants Elvis to have a good time in Vegas. Elvis likes and respects Frank.'

'So he'll go for it?'

'He'll just look at you as another potential buddy,' Parker said. 'He likes having people around him.'

'What about the others? How are they going to greet me?'

'I don't know,' he said. 'Maybe with suspicion. It'll be up to you to make them accept you.'

'How long is Elvis supposed to be in town?'

'A couple of weeks. He'll promote the movie, and do a few performances at the Riviera.'

'And where will you be all that time?'

'Right here. I have several new deals brewing and have to go over the contracts.'

'So if I need to talk to you...'

'...I'll be available, right here. Any time. Day or night.'

'Will you be here alone?'

'I will. I'll have someone bring in supplies

for me.' He picked up his glass and drained it.

'Cooking for yourself?'

'A little,' Parker said. 'I also have a freezer filled with TV dinners. I'll be fine. What do you say, Mr— Eddie. Eddie G., right? Is that what they call you?'

'That's right.'

'I'd really like you to do this,' Parker said. 'I can pay you well.'

'That won't be necessary, Colonel,' I said, standing up. 'I don't usually charge anyone for doing Frank Sinatra a favor.'

'I'd prefer to have you on the payroll,' he said. 'It would make our ... relationship clear.'

'I have one boss, Colonel,' I said. 'Jack Entratter at the Sands. I'll do this as a favor, or you'll have to get somebody else.'

Parker smiled. 'I never had anyone argue with me *not* to take my money.'

'Hey,' I said, spreading my hands, 'this is Vegas.'

FIVE

After seeing Colonel Parker and agreeing to 'chaperone' – for want of a better word – Elvis around Vegas I returned to my house and called the Sands, first to talk to Jack Entratter.

'So you agreed?' he asked.

'I agreed.'

'I knew it,' Entratter said. 'How long is this gonna keep you off the floor?'

'A couple of weeks, at least. Hopefully, that won't cause you too much trouble.'

'We'll try to get along without you, Eddie,' Jack said. 'By the way, where's Elvis gonna be staying?'

'The Riviera.'

Entratter made a rude sound with his mouth.

'Is he performing, also?'

'Yes,' I said, 'the Colonel said he's going to do a few shows.'

'All right,' Entratter said. I knew he had tried to get Elvis for the Sands a couple of times, and failed. He wasn't a happy camper. 'Stay in touch with me, Eddie. And let me know if you need anything.'

31

'I will, Jack.'

I hung up, called the Sands again and spoke to Frank.

'So Parker convinced you?' Frank said.

'He did.'

'Good,' Frank said. 'I know you'll keep the kid out of trouble.'

'Frank, I'll be on this job for about two weeks. You gonna be in town?'

'Not that long, but I told Elvis I'd come to his premier and bring the guys.'

'Dino?'

'And Sammy. Maybe Joey.'

'Peter?'

He didn't answer. He and Peter were still on the outs.

'I'm also gonna go to one of his shows, so yeah, I'll be around – although I'll be at the Cal Neva in Tahoe part of the time.'

'OK,' I said. 'Then I'll see you around.'

'Hey, Eddie?'

'Yeah?'

'Don't try to keep up with the kid,' he said. 'He can go all night. You ought to get some help, like your PI buddy, Bardini, or Jerry.'

'Maybe Jerry,' I said. 'He'd get a thrill out of meeting Elvis.'

'And Bardini wouldn't?'

'Not a fan,' I said. 'Talk to you soon, Frank.'

'See ya around, Clyde.'

After we hung up I decided to go out and get something to eat. I wanted a leisurely meal, over which I'd decide whether or not to import Jerry for this job. But before I could get out the door my phone rang.

'Eddie?'

'Hey, Danny.'

'Can you meet me at the Horseshoe?'

'Sure,' I said, 'I was about to get something to eat, anyway.'

'On me, then.'

'You must need me for a job real bad to buy,' I kidded.

'Not a job, Eddie,' Danny said. 'I need your help with something personal.'

He wasn't kidding around so I said, 'I'll be there, Danny. When?'

'Right now.'

SIX

The coffee shop at the Horseshoe was one of the best in town. It was also walking distance from Danny's Fremont Street office.

Danny Bardini was already sitting in a booth when I got there, with a cup of coffee in front of him. His hair was a mess and needed cutting, and his suit was wrinkled, as if he'd slept in it.

'Hey, Eddie,' he said, looking up at me. 'Thanks for coming.'

'It sounded important,' I said, sitting across from him.

'It is.'

The waitress came over and we both ordered a burger platter. It was easier than taking the time to study the menu. The food – though really good – was not the main reason we were there.

'What's going on, Danny?'

He took a moment to sip some coffee, then held the cup in both hands.

'OK, here it is,' he said. 'It's about Penny.'

'What about her?' I asked. 'Is she all right?'

34

Penny O'Grady was Danny's long-time secretary – Gal Friday, really – who had more than secretarial feelings for her boss. I believed it was the same for him, but he had never admitted it.

'Something's going on with her,' Danny said. 'She's been very ... secretive lately. Leaving early, coming in late. Unavailable in the evenings.'

'Have you asked her?'

'No.'

'Have you followed her?'

Danny hesitated, then said, 'No, I haven't. I–I can't do it.'

Uh-oh.

'But you can.'

'Danny—'

'Eddie,' he said, reaching across the table to grab my wrist, 'you gotta do this for me.'

'Why don't you just talk to her?'

'No,' he said, releasing my arm. 'If she wanted to talk to me she would have by now.'

'So what do you think is going on?'

'I don't know.'

Maybe he suspected she was seeing someone. Maybe he was coming to terms with his feelings for her.

'Danny, Penny's my friend.'

'I know, Eddie,' he said, 'that's why I'm asking you for help, and not somebody else. Because you're her friend ... and mine.'

My problem was I'd promised Frank and

Colonel Parker that I'd take care of Elvis. Now Danny was asking for a favor, and he'd been my friend a lot longer than anyone.

'OK, Danny,' I said, 'I'll see what I can find out. But I might need your help.' Putting him to work could keep his mind off Penny, and out of my way.

'What do you need?'

'I've agreed to do a favor for Frank,' I said. 'I'll need you to cover me.'

'What kind of trouble is he in now?'

'No trouble,' I said. 'Elvis Presley is coming to town...' I told him about my meetings with Entratter, Frank, and Colonel Parker.

'So they want you to babysit the King of Rock and Roll.'

'Pretty much.'

'And he's gonna have all these hangers-on around him?'

'All the time.'

'Why doesn't Parker get rid of them?' Danny asked. 'Word is he controls Elvis.'

'Not according to him,' I said. 'He says he's in charge of the financial end, but that Elvis makes his own decisions otherwise.'

'Interesting,' Danny said. 'When does he get here?'

'Two or three days,' I said. 'I'll have to check.'

'And what do you want me to do? Sit on him?'

'Just keep an eye on him,' I said. 'You know

the kinds of places in town he shouldn't go. The kinds of people he shouldn't associate with. Part of the job will be to keep him out of the newspapers.'

'And the other part is to keep him from goin' off the deep end?'

'Right.'

'OK,' he said. 'You find out what's goin' on with Penny for me, and I'll watch over the King for you. It's a deal.'

'Thanks,' I said. 'We have a few days. Maybe I'll find out what you want to know even before the King arrives.'

'Whatever,' he said. 'I'll do my part.'

The waitress came with our platters and set them down.

'Let's eat,' Danny said. 'I haven't had much of an appetite lately, but right now I'm pretty hungry.'

I nodded in agreement and repeated, 'Let's eat.'

SEVEN

I decided I needed Jerry.

One job I can handle but when it comes to two or more, Jerry's my guy. He hated being called a torpedo, but that was basically the job he performed in Brooklyn. Part of the reason we got along was that we were both from Brooklyn. He worked for Frank sometimes, and for mafia boss Momo Giancana, but in the four years I'd known him I'd come to depend on the fact that when I called him, he responded. Even if it meant getting on a plane at short notice, he came.

I went to the Sands and used an office phone to call him.

'You know I'll be there, Mr G.,' he said, after I'd explained. 'I like that Penny chick. She's too good for your friend the dick.' I knew he didn't mean that. He actually liked Danny.

'Jerry, I might use you on the Elvis thing, instead,' I said.

'That's fine with me if it's OK with him, Mr G. I wouldn't mind meetin' Elvis. I'll jump on the first plane.'

'I need you here in a couple of days, Jerry,' I told him. 'See if you can get a reasonably priced ticket. I'll cover it—'

'Hey,' Jerry said, 'don't sweat it, Mr G. I got it covered. I know how to get cheap tickets.'

'OK,' I said, 'let me know when you're landing. I'll pick you up if I can.'

'In the Caddy?'

'Yep,' I said, 'in the Caddy.'

'OK, Mr G.,' he said. 'I'll be seein' ya soon.'

I hung up the phone, looked up from the empty desk I was sitting at and saw Jack Entratter watching me.

'You'll cover the ticket?' he asked.

'Well ... you, me, it's all the same, Jack, when we're doing favors for the guys, right?'

He shook his head helplessly and walked to his own office. I didn't want to follow him because his girl always gave me disapproving looks when I went in there. After all these years I still don't know what I'd ever done to her.

I left the offices to head for the elevator when Jack's girl stuck her head out and said, 'Mr Gianelli?'

I turned. 'Yes.' I rarely – if ever – heard her use my name.

'You have a call.'

'Really?' I turned. 'Who is it?'

'He says,' she replied, 'that he's Elvis Presley...'

Well, it *was* Elvis Presley.

39

I had never expected my favor for Frank to take me to Memphis, and Graceland, and yet there I was, in front of the main gate.

As the limo I was in drove through the iron gates and up the long, winding driveway of Graceland, I ran the conversation through my mind, again...

'You want me to come there?' I asked. 'To Graceland?'

'That's right.' I don't know how Jack's girl could have doubted it. I recognized his voice. I was talking to Elvis Goddamn Presley! 'I'm more comfortable meeting new folks in a familiar environment. I'll send my plane for you, and then we can fly back to Vegas together.'

'Well...'

'Please, Mr Gianelli,' Elvis said. 'The Colonel says you're friends with Mr Sinatra. I like to think I'm friends with him, too. I wanna meet you as soon as possible, and this seems to be the quickest way. Besides, you'll have a good time.'

What could I say...

EIGHT

I rang the doorbell. It was opened by a big, beefy looking guy with red hair on his head and arms. I could hear music playing from somewhere inside.

'Yeah?'

'Eddie Gianelli,' I said. 'Elvis asked—'

'Come on in,' he said, cutting me off. 'I'll take you to him.'

He closed the door, turned to face me and stuck out his hand.

'Red West.'

'Eddie Gianelli,' I said. 'Or Eddie G.'

'OK,' he said, 'Eddie G. This way. Elvis is waitin' on you.'

He walked me through the house, which was full of people, a lot of them pretty girls in various states of undress. It was a party, all right, and in full swing, but there was no sign of Elvis.

To my right as I entered was the living room, dominated by a fifteen-foot white sofa. Beyond that double glass doors – with etched peacocks on them – led to the music room. I could see both a television set, and a baby grand piano.

To the left was the dining room, with a large table and not one, but two hutches. A large television set sat against one wall.

There was a stairway leading up, but we didn't go near it.

'Where is he?' I asked.

'He's on the firing range with some of the boys.'

'But ... what about his party?'

Red grinned and asked, 'What party?'

I followed Red down a hall, past a small kitchen where two women were apparently cooking a lot of food. On a far counter was a TV set, this one turned on.

The house was huge. I didn't know how many rooms there were, but it had to be over twenty. (I learned later there were twenty-three.) He had purchased it in 1957 when he was twenty-two, and paid $100,000. It had already bore the name Graceland, and Elvis liked it and kept it.

Red led me down a flight of steps and out a door into the backyard. It was there I first heard the gunshots.

'Elvis likes guns,' Red told me. 'He set up a shooting range back here so he could practice.'

I followed him until I saw a group of men laughing and brandishing guns. Elvis was in the center of them, firing at something. They were all laughing and shouting. I hoped they weren't drunk. I hated the thought of being around drunks with guns.

Elvis' hair was a mess as he fired and then whirled about for their approval. He was wearing a blue polo shirt, white chinos and shiny white shoes which I later discovered were patent leather.

One of the men looked enough like Red West to be his brother. I figured this was his cousin, Sonny.

'E!' Red shouted.

Elvis stopped whirling around and looked at us.

'He's here.'

Elvis held the gun in his right hand, pointed his left at me.

'Eddie G., right?'

'That's right.'

'Well, come on over here, son, and shake my hand.'

As I approached, he transferred the gun to his left hand and stuck out his right and then I shook hands with the King of Rock and Roll.

'These here are my boys,' he said, waving at the others. 'That there's Sonny West, Billy Smith, Lamar Fike and Marty Lacker. You already met Red.'

'I did,' I said. 'It's a real pleasure to meet you – all of you.'

'We were just blowing off some steam,' he said. 'You want to take a shot?'

I looked at the target, which was the figure of a man on a wooden board, with concentric circles inside it. A crude rendition of what you'd see on a police range, I supposed.

'No, thanks,' I said. 'I'm OK.'

'Red, you wanna take this?' Elvis handed over his gun, which looked a lot like one of Jerry's .45s. 'Me and Eddie are gonna walk over by the pool and have a talk.'

'Sure thing, E.' Red took the gun.

'You boys keep shootin',' he called out. 'I'll catch up later.' He put his arm around my shoulder and said, 'Come on, Eddie.'

He walked me a short way to a good-sized swimming pool. The water was clean, and there was no one using it at the moment.

'Is it OK if I call you Eddie? Or Eddie G.'

'Sure,' I said, 'why not?'

'And you call me Elvis, OK?'

'OK, Elvis.'

'I really appreciate you comin' out here.'

'Well, you sent a plane for me,' I said. 'Kind of hard to refuse.'

'I chartered that plane,' he said. 'Someday I'm gonna buy me one.'

'I'm wondering why you wanted me here badly enough to do that, Elvis.'

'I told you on the phone, Eddie,' he said. 'I like to meet folks face-to-face. When the Colonel told me about you I didn't want to wait until I got to Vegas. I thought if I brought you to my home we'd get to know each other better. Is that OK?'

'It's fine,' I said. 'Fine with me. This is a real

44

pleasure, to meet you and see your place.'

'That's good.'

'I do need to get myself a hotel room, though. I'll just have to—'

'Oh, na, na, na,' Elvis said, cutting me off, 'no hotel, Eddie. You're stayin' right here.'

'I don't want to impose.'

'You ain't imposin',' Elvis said. 'Hell, son, I invited you, didn't I? And we got plenty of room.'

'Really? I know it's a big house, but with all your, uh, buddies—'

'Oh, those guys are always here,' he said, 'but they don't live here. They got their own homes. Only my father, Vernon, lives with me. And he ain't here this week. He's visitin' some relatives. So we got the run of the whole house.'

'Is that why you're havin' the party?'

'What party?' he asked.

That's what Red had said, too.

'The people in the house...'

'Oh, that's not a party,' Elvis said. 'I just like having folks around. That's why one of my cooks is always in the kitchen.'

I wondered what the house looked like when there was a party going on?

'Come on,' he said, 'take some shots with the boys. I want them to get to know you, too.'

'Yeah, sure,' I said, 'why not? Let's shoot.'

'All right.' He slapped me on the back and beamed like a little boy. I'd made Elvis happy.

45

He turned and hurried back to the firing range, and I rushed to keep up.

'Lemme have that .45 for Eddie, Red!' he called out.

NINE

We shot targets for what seemed like most of the afternoon. Before long the Memphis Mafia was slapping me on the back and kidding around. The only one who never cracked a smile was Red West. In fact, I had the feeling Red didn't ever look happy. He appeared to be a few years older than Elvis, a burly guy with a marine crew cut that hinted at the reason he was called 'Red', and a bulldog face.

When we were done Elvis and the guys collected spent cartridges from the ground.

'While we clean up, Red'll show you where your room is, Eddie. You can get cleaned up and then Red'll bring you back down.'

'OK, Elvis.'

'You hear, Red?' he said.

'Sure thing, E.,' Red said. He looked at me. 'Come on.'

I followed Red back into the house, through the party that wasn't a party, to the staircase, and up to the second floor.

'E. don't usually let nobody up here,' Red told me.

'I'm honored.'

'You should be.'

When we got upstairs away from the noise I asked, 'What do you have against me, Red?'

'I ain't got nothin' against you,' Red said. 'I just don't like folks moochin' offa Elvis.'

'What makes you think I'm mooching off him?'

'You flew in his plane, didn'tcha? Gonna be sleepin' in his house tonight? Eatin' his food?'

'And none of that was my idea,' I informed him. 'I was invited here, Red.'

'So were all those moochers downstairs. This is your room.'

We stopped in front of the open door. I saw my suitcase on the double bed.

'So you mean all those folks downstairs, and me, are moochers,' I said, 'unlike you and the rest of the Memphis crew.'

He bristled at that, his face glowing red, and said, 'We're his friends.' He glared at me. 'I'll come and get ya when Elvis tells me to.'

'Yeah, fine.'

He turned and left, his shoulders hunched. He probably wanted to pummel me, but Elvis wouldn't have liked it. I wondered how many of the Memphis Mafia were like Red West?

My room had its own bathroom, so I was able to clean myself up and change into a fresh shirt. As I was buttoning it up there was a knock on the door. It was Red.

'Elvis wants you.'

'Sure,' I said. 'Lead the way.'

We went down the hall and as we reached the stairway I became aware of the quiet.

'Everybody gone?' I asked.

'Yeah,' he said, 'Elvis told them to go home. It's just gonna be the fellas tonight.'

We went past the kitchen, where a cook – a middle-aged woman – was moving around, tending to pots and pans on the stove. I could hear something sizzling in a pan, and the smells coming from there made my stomach growl.

'Where we going?' I asked.

'E.'s in the TV room.'

'There's a TV room?'

'You'll see.'

I followed him down toward the basement. When we got to the bottom of the stairs I saw a pool table off to the right, where four of the guys were shooting a game. Red turned left and I followed him.

Red went into the room first, blocking my view. It wasn't until I actually entered that I saw Elvis sitting on a sofa in front of three television sets, all of which were turned on, with a different station on each.

Elvis was holding a half-eaten banana and peanut butter sandwich in one hand, and silver-plated gun in the other. On the coffee table in front of him was a bowl of assorted fruits, a plate of what looked like fudge cookies, and a box of cigars, El Producto Diamond Tips.

'Eddie.' Elvis stood up, but waited for me to approach him so we could shake hands again. He had changed, but was still wearing white pants and a polo shirt, this one pale yellow with a high collar.

I looked at the televisions to see what he was watching. Three different news shows blared on.

'How do you like the layout?'

'That's a whole lot of TVs.' I said.

'You know, I heard Lyndon Johnson keeps three sets on at all times, watches all the network news shows at once. I figured if it's good enough for the President, it's good enough for me.'

'Sounds fair.'

'Have a seat,' he said, sitting back on the U-shaped green sofa. 'Have some fruit, or cookies. We're gonna be eatin' soon. Want somethin' to drink? Pepsi? We got orange drinks. Red, we got any beer?'

'I think so,' Red said.

'Whataya have, Eddie?' Elvis asked.

'I'll have what you're having.'

'Pepsi,' Elvis said, 'Red, get Eddie a Pepsi, will you?'

'Sure thing, E.'

Red exited the room, and I was alone with Elvis, and his gun. He had set the sandwich down on the table to shake hands, but he still gripped the gun in his left hand. I could hear

50

the pool balls clanking in the other room.

'The guys are shootin' some pool before we eat,' Elvis said.

'Will they be coming to Vegas?' I asked.

'Oh, yeah,' he said, 'most of my boys will be comin'. What about Frank? Is he in Vegas now?'

'Yes,' I said, 'he says he's gonna go to your show.'

'Great!' Elvis said. 'I'll introduce him to the crowd. He's a real star.'

Elvis calling Frank Sinatra a real star? I wondered what Elvis considered himself to be?

Red West came back in at that point, carrying a cold can of Pepsi, and handed it to me.

'Cook says the chicken fried steak's almost ready, E.,' Red said. 'And the meat loaf.'

'OK, Red.'

Elvis leaned forward, picked up a fudge cookie and shoved it into his mouth.

'OK, Eddie,' he said, 'sit down and tell me the Eddie G. story. How'd you end up in Vegas?'

'I was born in Brooklyn...'

We talked for a while about how I got to Vegas, learned the city, got it wired, how I had met Frank, Dino and Sammy, and all the while he held onto the gun, sometimes twirling it like a six-shooter. Once or twice he pointed it at the TV, and I thought he was going to pull the trigger.

'You hungry, Eddie?' he asked, suddenly.

'I could eat,' I said, although nothing on the coffee table was tempting me.

'Red, tell the cook to bring the food down here, will ya?'

'Sure thing, E.'

'And get some of the boys to help her carry it!' he called after him. 'You're gonna love this food, Eddie. I got the best cooks in Memphis.'

TEN

It was Red and his cousin Sonny who brought the food down, plates of it, and another man I hadn't seen before.

'Hey, Eddie,' Elvis said, 'meet my buddy, Nick Adams.'

Adams turned to me, holding a platter of chicken fried steaks. He was short, blond, not handsome, but with an easy, charming smile. I knew where I'd seen him before. He was TV's *The Rebel*, Johnny Yuma.

'Hey,' he said, extending his hand, 'nice to meet you.'

'Same here,' I said. 'I've seen your show.'

'Whoa,' Adams said, looking at Elvis and grinning, 'you notice he said he's seen the show, not that he liked it.' He set the platter down on the big coffee table in front of the sofa. Red set down a platter of meat loaf right next to it, and Sonny added the vegetables.

'I'll get some plates and forks and stuff,' he said, rushing from the room.

'I liked it well enough,' I said, 'just not as much as *Wanted: Dead or Alive* or *Have Gun*

Will Travel.'

'Really good shows,' Adams said. 'Hey, I did *Hell Is For Heroes* with Steve.'

'Bobby Darin, too,' I said. I looked at Elvis. 'Bobby's playing Vegas right now.'

'That's great, son,' Elvis said. 'We can catch his show. Red, tell the guys to come and eat.'

Red went into the pool room and came back with Billy Smith, Lamar Fike and Marty Lacker. Sonny came in behind them with a stack of dishes and a handful of knives and forks.

'Dig in, boys!' Elvis said. And – as they say in the South – we commenced to eating.

'We hear you're gonna show us a good time in Vegas,' Sonny said.

'I'm going to give it a good try,' I promised. I looked at Adams. 'Are you coming, too?'

'Naw, I got work to do,' he said. 'I'm doin' an episode of *The Outer Limits*.'

'But for tonight,' Elvis said, 'he's here. We're all gonna watch a movie on TV. But first dessert, up in the kitchen. The cook made a big bowl of banana pudding. Come on!'

Elvis bounded up off the sofa, bouncing on the balls of his feet. His eyes were shining. His pupils like pin pricks. He sprang out the door, followed by the others. I looked at Red, who had remained in the room, presumably to escort me.

'Another moocher,' he said, as we went out the door.

* * *

We watched a couple of John Wayne westerns, everybody laughing and joking, drinking beer or Pepsi, eating popcorn, brownies, cookies. I didn't watch the movies, I watched the people, the Memphis Mafia and how they interacted with Elvis.

I could see Elvis trying to act like one of the guys, and I could see the others trying to pretend like he was, but they all knew he wasn't. To me the whole relationship looked like it took a lot of effort, but then I had only been around them a short time. Maybe this was normal and they all loved each other, and him. Maybe the fact that he was rich and paying for everything had nothing to do with it.

Maybe I was just a cynic.

I was relieved to see that Elvis watched the two movies without the .45 in his hand.

I ate popcorn and drank soda with the Memphis Mafia, and when the movies were over they began to drift away. Elvis had said they all had their own homes, but some of them could have gone to other bedrooms in the house. Eventually, I was left there when the lights came back on, with Red and Sonny West, and Elvis.

'See that?' Elvis said, pointing at the TV. He seemed agitated.

'What?' I asked, not even really sure he was talking to me, or to them.

'John Wayne,' Elvis said. 'Nobody ever said he can't act just because he's John Wayne.

They say I can't do drama because people will always see Elvis Presley.'

'They're wrong, E.,' Red West said.

'Damn straight they're wrong,' Sonny said. They all looked at me.

'I thought you did great in *Flaming Star*,' I offered.

'Yeah, that was one of my favorites,' he said, 'but I want to do a real good western, you know? The kind of movie John Wayne would be proud of? They want me to keep doing these Hal Wallis movies with the girls.'

Elvis and music and girls had been a pretty good formula for the studio up til now. I didn't blame them for wanting to keep their cash cow going, but why not throw him a serious movie or two? Wasn't that what the Colonel was supposed to be doing for him?

'Is your room ok?' Elvis asked. Suddenly his mood changed and he was no longer agitated.

'It's fine, Elvis,' I said. 'Very comfortable.'

'Well,' he said, 'you're used to those fancy suites in Vegas.'

'Not me,' I said. 'I have my own house, a hell of a lot smaller than this, but comfortable for me.'

'Really?' he said. 'You got a house in Las Vegas? I thought all you casino fellas lived in the casino hotel.'

'Not many do,' I said. 'That's where we work, not where we live.'

'Well, I'll be danged,' he said. 'I'd like to see

your house.'

'Oh, well, it wouldn't impress you—'

'You shoulda seen the house I grew up in, in Tupelo,' Elvis said. 'I think yours will be just fine.'

'Well...' I said, again. 'Yeah, we can do that.'

'Good!' he said, leaping to his feet happily.

'Time to turn in, E.,' Sonny said.

Elvis didn't argue. 'I'll see you in the mornin', Eddie. You want anythin' durin' the night you just go down to the kitchen and get it. You want somethin' cooked, somebody'll be there to cook it for ya.'

'Thanks, Elvis.'

''night, Eddie G.'

He left the room with Sonny. Red stayed behind me, staring at me balefully.

'I can find my way to my room, Red.'

'Elvis wants me to show you.'

'Sure.'

I got up and followed Red through the first floor which was strewn with the debris of the party that wasn't a party. I wondered whose job it would be to clean it up? Considering everything I'd seen Red do so far, it wouldn't have surprised me if he was responsible.

ELEVEN

I woke early, dressed and came downstairs, carrying my overnight bag. I was surprised to find Elvis in the kitchen, having breakfast.

'Hey, Eddie,' he said. He wasn't wearing the same exact clothes, but it looked like a duplicate of the earlier pants and shirt. His shoes were white tennis shoes. He was standing at the stove, watching the cook work her magic. The pans were filled with scrambled eggs, potatoes, both bacon and sausage.

'There's coffee, there,' he said, indicating a pot on the stove. 'Get a cup and bring it to the dining room. Cups right above there.'

I opened a cabinet above the coffee pot and took down a cup, poured it full, then went out to the dining room, where he was sitting at the table.

'When does the plane leave to go back to Vegas?' I asked, sitting across from him.

'You tell me. It's up to you.'

'Well, I need to get back to make ... arrangements.'

'I'd ask you to stay another day,' he said, 'but

I got business, too. Frank tell you why I'm goin' to Vegas?'

'For the opening of *Viva Las Vegas*,' I said. 'To promote it.'

'That's right,' he said. 'I should be in LA shooting *Kissin' Cousins*, but the Colonel got me a couple of weeks to go to Vegas.'

'He also told me Ann-Margret would be there.'

His face softened at the mention of Ann-Margret. I knew they had been linked outside of *Viva Las Vegas*, and that had probably caused him some trouble with Priscilla. They were planning to be married once she graduated from high school. I didn't really understand that relationship, but then I didn't know all the details. I assumed – since I hadn't seen her and she hadn't been mentioned – that she was also away, like his father.

'She really wants to meet Frank,' he said. 'She's a sweet kid.'

'I can arrange that, if you like,' I said, 'but you can probably do it yourself.'

'Na, na, na,' he said, 'you're Eddie G., you're the man. I'll introduce you to her, and you get her to Frank. How's that?'

'Sounds good to me, Elvis.'

The cook came out and set platters of food in front of us. Elvis attacked the meal with gusto. His hair was slick and shiny, every strand in place. I was amazed at how clear and smooth his skin was, as if he never had to shave. On his

59

next birthday he'd be thirty, I figured, but he looked a lot younger than that at the moment.

'I'll have the limo take you to the plane when you finish your breakfast,' Elvis said. 'Red'll let you know when it's here.'

'Just so you know, Elvis,' I said, 'Red doesn't like me much.'

He laughed, paused with a forkful of food halfway to his mouth. I figured he must burn a lot of energy, because ever since my arrival it seemed he was always eating something.

'Son,' he said, 'Red don't like anybody. Don't worry about it. I like you. That's all that matters.' He slapped me on the back then and added, 'See ya in Vegas.'

'Soon,' I said.

He smiled again, like a happy kid.

I sat at the table after Elvis left, finishing my coffee – which was excellent, by the way – wondering again about him and his Memphis Mafia? His friends, or a bunch of enablers and moochers? Maybe the guy to ask about that was Red West. But I doubted Red would tell me anything, not at this stage in our 'relationship'.

I had almost mentioned Danny to him, but since I wasn't sure how much I'd be using Danny I decided to put that off until another time.

Red appeared, wearing a T-shirt and grey slacks.

'Time to go to the plane,' he said.

'Thanks, Red.'

'Don't thank me,' he said. 'I'm just doin' what E. wants me to do.'

'Well,' I said, 'thanks anyway. I think we got off on the wrong foot. Maybe I can change that when you get to my town.'

He stared at me for a minute, then said, 'Car's outside,' turned, and left.

Or maybe not.

TWELVE

When we touched down in Vegas I caught a cab back to my house. I took a shower, processing what I had found out in Memphis. Elvis was a nice guy. That's the impression I got. He kept a lot of people around him, and took care of them, but they also took care of him. I thought Red West would do just about anything Elvis asked him to do. Maybe that went for the rest of the MM, too, but I'd need to see more of them to know for sure.

The only thing that bothered me was the way Elvis' eyes looked to me that night. Drugs? I'd say yes, but I couldn't guess what kind. Did all drugs make pinpricks of your pupils or only some? I'd need to talk to an expert for the answer.

After the shower I dressed casually, because I wasn't going into work. No suits when I was away from the Sands. Sports shirt, grey slacks, loafers. Now that I was back I needed to do something about finding out what Penny was up to.

I called Danny and he told me that Penny was in the office and supposed to stay there and do some paperwork. He said he had to go out on a case; I told him to go ahead. For what I had to do, I didn't need him.

What I had to do was follow Penny when she left the office. I didn't like the idea of spying on her. She was my friend. They both were. But maybe she had a problem she couldn't talk to Danny about. Maybe she would be able to discuss it with me.

I got in my Caddy and drove to Fremont Street.

Danny's office was a few doors down from the Horseshoe.

I parked behind the casino, so that Penny wouldn't spot my car. I hadn't made up my mind yet how I was going to handle things. Should I confront her, or follow her first?

Penny answered the question for me. As I was walking down the street she came out the door and – luckily – started up the street away from me. I had no choice but to follow her on foot.

She walked a few blocks and then caught a cab in front of the Golden Nugget. Again luck was with me, because it was a cab stand and I was able to grab another one right away.

'Follow that cab,' I said.

'Are you kiddin' me?'

'Save the cracks,' I said. 'Drive.'

'Whatever you say.'

I settled back and tried not to yell at the cab driver each time I thought he was going to lose her.

Penny went to the post office, the bank and the grocery store. Maybe she decided to do her paperwork another day. Or maybe she got it all done early and realized she could run errands. Whatever the reason, after the grocery store she had the cab driver take her right home to her apartment.

'Now what?' the cabbie asked, as we parked in front of her building.

'For you, nothing,' I said, paying him. 'For me, who knows?'

I opened the door to get out and he said, 'You mind some advice?'

'Sure, why not? Go ahead.'

'Talk to the girl,' he said. 'To me, it don't look like she's doin' what you think she's doin'.'

I hesitated, didn't say the first thing that came to my mind, and then said, 'I'll keep that in mind. Thanks.'

'Just tryin' to help.'

He drove off and I looked around for a likely place to watch from. I had been to Penny's place a few times, but not recently. I was surprised to see a small restaurant across the street. I quickly crossed and went inside, got a table near the window and checked the menu. I was hungry.

I ordered a burger platter, keeping my eyes on Penny's building, hoping she wouldn't come out again before I finished eating.

The building had eight floors, and I knew Penny's apartment was on the fifth, in the front. I thought I had her window spotted, and there was a light on.

There could have already been someone waiting for her in her apartment. Other people entered the building, some of them men. One of them could have been going in to see her. There would be no fear of being seen, really, because she wouldn't really be cheating on Danny. He knew how she felt about him, and was dopey enough to keep her at arm's length. If she wanted to have a guy visit her at home, that was up to her. Maybe she'd gone shopping to cook the guy a meal. She'd come out of the store with only two paper bags of groceries, certainly enough to prepare a meal.

I finished my burger and fries – burger over-done, fries kinda limp – and washed it down with a Coke. It started to get dark, and she still didn't come out. I was getting impatient.

I finally decided to pack it in, and try again the next day. I had started the day in Memphis, and had been on the go since getting off the plane in Vegas. I was tired and decided to go home.

I paid the check, left the restaurant and could not find a cab until I walked a few blocks. I had him take me to the rear of the Horseshoe, where I reclaimed my Caddy and drove home.

I had stopped off at a bakery I liked and picked up some pastries, and was eating them with coffee when my phone rang. I still missed the Italian bakeries of Brooklyn, but this one I had found was pretty good.

'Hello?'

'It's me, Mr G.,' Jerry said. 'I'll be on a plane tomorrow, gettin' in at noon. That OK?'

'That's great, Jerry,' I said. 'I'll pick you up.'

'In the Caddy?'

'Yup, in the Caddy.'

'Then can we go to the diner in the Horseshoe?' he asked, hopefully.

'Jerry,' I said, 'that's exactly where I intended to go.'

THIRTEEN

I was waiting for Jerry when he came in off the tarmac. We collected his suitcase from baggage claim and I didn't try to take it from him, because I knew from experience it'd be too heavy for me. Jerry traveled 'light' by taking one suitcase wherever he went, but there was nothing 'light' about it. He used a large case, and he packed it full.

He tossed the suitcase into the back seat of the Caddy, like it was a feather, and slid happily behind the wheel.

'The Horseshoe?' he asked.

'The Horseshoe,' I said. 'Know the way?'

He grinned and said, 'I'll follow my nose.'

'What's with the houndstooth jacket?' I asked as we started out.

'I'm tryin to update my wardrobe,' he said. 'You don't like it?'

'Well ... you're a big guy, Jerry, and that makes for a lot of houndstooth. Besides, it'll be too hot for that in the day time.'

'Then I'll wear it at night.'

He drove directly to the Horseshoe with no

wrong turns and we parked in the back. Along the way he asked about Frank, Dino and Sammy and when I'd last seen them in Vegas. I told him Frank was here now.

As we got out of the car to go inside he said, 'How about the dick? He meetin' us to eat?'

'He's one of the things we have to talk about, Jerry,' I answered.

'And Elvis?'

I nodded. 'And Elvis.'

When we got into the coffee shop we took a booth – which was able to accommodate his bulk – and he ordered a super stack of pancakes with a side of bacon, coffee and orange juice. I ordered some toast and coffee.

'That's all you're eatin'?'

'I had breakfast at home.'

'So, what's goin' on, Mr G.?' he asked. 'Sounds like we got some problems.'

I laid it all out for him, my agreement to do a favor for Frank, and a favor for Danny. While I was talking the waitress came over with the food, laid it down and he started plowing through it, but that didn't stop him from catching every word.

'So how do you wanna do this, Mr G?' he asked, when I was done. 'You want me on Elvis, or you want me to follow the girl?'

'I've known Danny since I was a kid in Brooklyn, Jerry,' I said. 'I feel like I should be helping him.'

'Then I'll hang out with Elvis.'

'I don't think that would sit well with Frank, or the Colonel, or Elvis,' I said. 'As far as Elvis knows, I'm supposed to be showing him a good time in Vegas.'

Jerry frowned. 'Don't know if I could do that.'

'So I guess you should follow Penny,' I said.

'Do I get to use the Caddy?'

'Yeah,' I said. 'I'll use cabs, or borrow a car. Or, if I know Elvis at this point, we'll have a limo.'

'OK.'

'But Elvis isn't here yet,' I said. 'So I think today we'll both shadow Penny and see what's up. I followed her yesterday, but all she did was run errands.'

'Did you watch her place to see if she got any visitors?'

'I did,' I said. 'I don't think she had any, unless someone came by much later last night.'

'If we're thinkin' she's got a guy, maybe that's what happened,' Jerry suggested.

'Then maybe one of us needs to stay outside her place a lot later tonight.'

'Why do I think that's gonna be me?'

'I'll get you a suite at the Sands while you're here,' I said. 'But I think you're gonna be getting there very late tonight.'

'Whatever you say, Mr G.'

'Today's a work day,' I said. 'She should be in the office.'

'And the dick?'

'He's working on a case, so he should be out.'

'Did he ever think of, you know, just askin' her what's goin' on?'

'Yeah, I don't think he wants to do that.'

He finished his last bite of bacon, washed it down with the last of his coffee.

'I'm ready,' he said.

'There's an arcade across the street from Danny's office,' I said. 'We can watch from there, wait and see if she comes out.'

'Ain't I gonna stand out in an arcade?'

I smiled at him and said, 'Not on Fremont Street, big fella.'

FOURTEEN

We left the Horseshoe, crossed the street and walked to the arcade. It was not the kind of arcade you would see small kids in. There were bells, whistles, lights, street walkers, hustlers, homeless people and the occasional tourist who had wandered in carrying gross misconceptions with them. Not a pinball machine in the place, with some dubious items up for sale.

'Hey big boy,' a teenage hooker said to Jerry, 'lookin' for somethin' to do?'

'Get lost, honey,' he growled at her in a tone that had her scampering away.

We took up positions on either side of the entrance, from where we could easily see the front of Danny's building, and the doorway to his office.

Some of the pickpockets who were taking a break from working the casino crowds decided to leave when they saw us, probably thinking we were cops. That actually worked in our favor, keeping any of the other street girls from approaching us.

After about forty minutes Danny came out

71

the door. I checked the window that over-
looked the street and didn't see Penny there, so
I stepped out and waved at him.

'Hey, big guy,' he said, when he saw Jerry.
'Shamus.'

'What's he doin' here?' he asked me, keeping
his voice low.

'I'm gonna use him for the Elvis thing,' I
said. He nodded, accepting that. 'Is Penny inside?'

'Yeah. Did you follow her yesterday?'

'I did, but all she did was run errands and
grocery shop.'

'She's not very talkative today,' he said.
'That's another tip-off that somethin's goin'
on.'

'Danny, what about just askin' her?'

'You could do that, maybe,' he said. 'Not me.
She'd think I don't trust her.'

I didn't point out that it seemed like he didn't.

'What's on the agenda today?' I asked.

'Same as yesterday,' he said. 'She's supposed
to do some paperwork and stay in.'

'And you?'

'I'll be gone all day.'

On the spur of the moment I said, 'Give me a
key to the office.'

'Why?'

'I want to take a look at her desk.'

'Yeah, OK.' He took two keys off his key
ring, one for the downstairs door, and one for
the door to the office.

'OK,' I said. 'I'll be in touch.'

Danny tossed Jerry a wave and took off. I walked over to stand next to Jerry.

'I'm gonna get the car and bring it around the corner. Yesterday I got lucky and found a cab. I don't want to take that chance today.'

'OK.'

'I won't be long, but if she comes out while I'm gone, tail her.'

'OK, Mr G.'

I left the arcade and rushed to the rear of the Horseshoe to bring the Caddy around. When I got back to the arcade my heart sank. Jerry was gone. Penny must have wasted no time after Danny left. I took a quick look up and down the block, hoping to spot Jerry's houndstooth coat, but to no avail.

They were gone.

I let myself into the offices of Bardini Investigations.

Penny's desk was right out front. The door to Danny's office was open, and I could see a mess on top of his desk, but that was his business. I crossed the room and sat myself down behind Penny's desk. I went through the drawers, found a lot of candy but otherwise nothing incriminating. I checked her calendar, which was meant to hold appointments for Danny. I checked the past month, though, to see if she might have made some notes for herself. I found a few references to someone with the initials R.F. I wrote down the initials, the dates and times in a small notebook I carried. I went through her Rolodex, did not find any numbers for someone with those initials. Before leaving, I checked the top of her desk, including her blotter. Not finding anything tucked into the sides, I lifted it and peered underneath. There I found a slip of paper with a series of numbers on it. The grouping told me it was not a phone number. I wrote them down in my notebook.

I did a quick circuit of the room, didn't find anything on the walls or the tops of the file cabinets. The last thing I did was check the wall calendar. Obviously, she made all her notations on her desk calendar.

I left the office, careful to lock the door behind me. When I got down to the street I peered out first to make sure I didn't walk into Penny, then stepped out and locked that one, as well.

There was nothing else I could do about Penny except wait to hear from poor Jerry, who was on foot and didn't even know if he had a hotel room yet. I decided to go to the Sands and make sure that when he needed it, he did.

FIFTEEN

At the Sands I went right to the front desk and arranged a suite for Jerry. Then I had a bell boy – one of the bigger ones the hotel had – take his bag up to it.

After that I took the elevator to the office floor. I figured if Jerry was going to call me he'd call Entratter's office and leave a message. That meant I had to check with Jack's girl, who hated me.

As I entered the outer office she gave that look she reserved especially for me. I never try to describe it. I just know it always made me feel cold inside.

'I was wondering if you had any phone messages here for me?'

'No,' she said, coldly.

'Is Jack in?'

'Yes.' She picked up her phone. 'Mr Gianelli is here.' She hung up. 'Go in.'

'Thanks.'

I shook off the icicles and entered Jack's office.

'What's going on?' Entratter asked as I

approached his desk.

'Can I sit?'

'Go ahead,' Entratter said. He had a cup of coffee at his elbow. 'Want somethin'?'

'No,' I said, 'I won't be here that long. I was really just checking for messages.'

He raised his eyebrows. 'Are we your message center now?'

'I lost contact with Jerry,' I said. 'I thought he might call here to check in.'

'You talk to the girl?' I don't think I had ever heard her name. I could be wrong.

'I did,' I said. 'I got no message and the cold shoulder.'

'What are you and Jerry doin'?' Entratter asked. 'Elvis ain't in town yet, is he?'

'No,' I said. 'I think he might be coming tomorrow, but I haven't heard, yet.'

'Should I alert my girl to take that message, too?' he asked.

I almost said no, but instead said, 'You know, maybe you should.' I wondered what the Ice Lady would do if she picked up the phone and Elvis Presley was on the other end, again?

'Yeah, I suppose so,' he grumbled. 'What about the Colonel?'

'Still on the lake, I guess.'

'And Frank?'

'In his suite,' I guessed. 'He says he's gonna hang around to go to Elvis' show.'

'That should be interesting.'

'Yeah, Elvis says he's gonna introduce

76

Frank.'

'*That* should be interesting,' Jack said again, with a different inflection.

Entratter's phone rang several times, but his girl did the answering.

'So why are you still here?' he asked.

That was my cue. I stood up.

'Keep me up to date on where you are and what you're doin', Eddie,' Jack said. 'And try to stay out of jail.'

'What's that supposed to mean?'

'That means that when you and Jerry and your friend Danny mix, one of you always ends up in jail.'

I couldn't argue with that.

But...

'What makes you think Danny's involved?'

'History,' Entratter said.

I couldn't argue with that, either.

'I'm out of here,' I said.

'Good,' he said, and turned his attention back to whatever was on his desk.

When I got to the outer office his girl looked up at me. She seemed to have something to say, and was unhappy about it.

'You do have a telephone message, Mr Gianelli,' she said. 'It came in while you were with Mr Entratter.'

'Thank you,' I said. I waited, and she finally handed me a slip of paper from a pink message pad, with a pained look on her pretty-but-stern face.

That done, she immediately put me out of her mind.

I took the message out to the hall with me, just to get to a warmer climate. I looked at the slip, expecting it to be from Jerry. It wasn't.

'Please come to my suite as soon as you get this,' it read.

Underneath was the name of the person who had left the message: Frank Sinatra.

I went directly to the elevators and took one to Frank's floor. When the Chairman of the Board calls, you answer.

SIXTEEN

This time when Frank offered me a drink I accepted. In minutes we each had a bourbon in our hands, although Frank would have preferred a Martini or a Manhattan.

'I heard from the Colonel,' Frank said, leaning on his side of the bar. 'So far he's pretty happy with you.'

'Is he?' I asked. 'I haven't done anything, yet.'

'He heard you went to Graceland,' Frank said. 'Elvis liked you. What did you do there?'

'We shot targets, ate, and watched movies.'

'Interesting,' Frank said, sipping his drink. 'I've never been there.'

I didn't know what to say to that, so I sipped my drink, too.

'The Colonel said that Elvis is comin' in tomorrow.'

'I thought one of them would call and let me know,' I said.

'Parker said Elvis tried to call you at home,' Frank said. 'So the Colonel decided to call me and leave you a message.'

Apparently Frank didn't object to being a message center the way Entratter did.

'He'll be at the Riviera,' Frank went on.

'I'll call the hotel and see when he's gettin' in,' I said. 'I'll be there.'

Frank eyed me for a minute and then said, 'What's goin' on?'

'What do you mean?'

'There's somethin' else on your mind besides Elvis Presley.'

'What makes you say that?'

'Come on, Eddie,' Frank said. 'We've been friends long enough. I can tell when my friends have somethin' on their minds.'

'Speaking of friends I heard Dino's comin' to town,' I said.

'Don't change the subject.'

Caught.

'My buddy Danny Bardini's havin' some trouble and I promised to help him out.'

'So you'll have to split your time between Elvis and Danny?'

'Looks like.'

'Get some help,' he suggested. 'I'll fly Jerry in for you, if you want.'

'Actually, Jerry's here and he's already on the job.'

'Well, that's good.'

'It should be, but I've already lost track of him.'

'He'll turn up,' Frank said. 'Jerry can take care of himself.'

'I know that,' I said, 'it's just that he hasn't even had time to settle in, yet.'

'Well,' Frank said, 'you've got the rest of the day to find him and make your arrangements for tomorrow.'

'Then I better get to it.'

I sipped the drink again and put the glass down. Frank walked me to the door with his arm around my shoulder.

'Let me know if you need any help,' he said, as we opened the door, 'with either problem. I'm available.'

'I'll remember that, Frank.'

'And yes, Dino is comin' in. In fact, he'll be here tomorrow night.'

'Good,' I said, 'I haven't seen him in a while.'

'Let's try to all have dinner,' Frank said, 'if you can squeeze us in.'

'I'll try,' I promised.

'See ya, Eddie.'

He closed the door and I went to the elevator. I had the rest of the day to find Jerry, and had no idea where to look.

SEVENTEEN

I went down to the lobby and checked with the front desk for messages. Finding none, I asked the desk clerk – who had the name 'DEREK' on his name tag – 'Can I use your phone?'

'Sure, Mr G.'

He turned the phone around to me so I could make an outside call. I knew if Elvis was checking into the Riviera the next day they'd know exactly when he was coming in. I knew the concierge at the Riviera because he had once worked at the Sands.

'Hey, Eddie G.,' Tommy Harper said, glad to hear my voice. 'What's shakin'?'

'Hey, Tommy, how you doin'?'

'Can't complain,' Harper said. 'What can I do for you?'

'I need a favor, man.'

'Sure, anything,' Tommy said. 'But I can't believe that Eddie G., who's got this whole town wired, needs my help.'

'This has to do with a famous guest of yours,' I told him.

'Uh-oh,' he said, lowering his voice to a conspiratorial tone, 'don't tell me it's about Elvis Presley.'

'It is.'

'Eddie, man,' he said, 'I can't give out any information about that.'

'I'm supposed to meet with him at your hotel,' I said. 'I only need to know when he's comin' in. He tried to call me at home and I wasn't there.'

'Elvis calls you at home?'

'This would've been the first time, but yeah.'

He hesitated, then asked, 'Is this on the level, Eddie? Because it could cost me my job.'

'It won't,' I said. 'It's totally on the level. All I need is his time of arrival, so I know when to be there myself.'

He hesitated again, then said – lowering his voice – 'OK, it's noon. He's due to check in at noon.'

'Thanks, Tommy.'

'Don't hang me out to dry, Eddie,' he said. 'If I see photographers here—'

'You won't,' I said. 'Not because of me, any-way.'

'Yeah, I know,' Harper said, 'it'll leak out, anyway, but...'

'I won't say a word, Tommy,' I promised. 'I swear.'

'OK, Eddie.'

'Thanks for helpin' me out,' I said. 'Now I owe you one.'

'I'll call it in,' Harper said. 'Take care.'

I hung up and said to Derek, 'Thanks for the use of the phone.'

'Any time, Mr G.,' he said. 'Hey, how come they don't give you an office?'

'Pit bosses don't get offices,' I said, 'but thanks for the thought.'

I took a walk through the casino floor, exchanged some greetings with Red Skelton, who was not playing the Sands but had chosen to gamble there, and Alan King, who was watching.

I went to the Garden Room for coffee, then checked back with the desk for messages. I was hoping Jerry would simply call the hotel, and not Jack Entratter's number. Or maybe he'd call Frank, who would then call down to the desk looking for me.

I went back to the Garden Room and decided to have a piece of pie this time with my coffee. I was finishing the last bite when the waitress came over with a phone, plugged it in and set it down on the table.

'A call for you, Eddie.'

'Thanks, Kitty.'

She smiled and walked away. I watched her swaying butt as I picked up the receiver.

'Yeah, this is Eddie.'

'I told you,' Jack Entratter said, 'didn't I tell you?'

'Tell me what, Jack?'

'Your buddy Jerry called here lookin' for

84

you.'

'You should've told him to call down to the front desk,' I said. 'He would've found me.'

'Well, he couldn't do that,' Jack said. 'You see, he's only allowed one phone call.'

'One call?'

'That's right,' Jack said. 'He's in jail.'

I closed my eyes and thought, Jesus.

'For what?' I asked.

'No half measures for your good buddy,' Jack said. 'He's been arrested and charged with murder!'

EIGHTEEN

Detective Hargrove had a self-satisfied look on his face as he came to fetch me from the front hall of police headquarters.

'So, one of you finally did it, huh, Eddie?' he asked.

'I'll need to see the evidence, detective, before I agree to that.'

The look slipped and I knew he didn't have the evidence he needed to make the charge stick.

'Come with me,' he said.

I followed him down several familiar halls. We were headed for the interrogation rooms. I'd been in them enough times before to know.

He stopped in front of a door and turned to face me.

'OK, your buddy's inside,' he said. 'It would benefit him if you could get him to talk.'

'Benefit you, you mean.'

'You want to talk to him, or not?'

'I do.'

'Then be smart, Eddie,' Hargrove said. 'I knew one of you would slip up one day. I sort of hoped it would be you, though.'

He opened the door and allowed me to enter the room.

'Hey, Mr G.,' Jerry said. He was sitting at an interview table, and I noticed he was not handcuffed.

'Hey, Jerry,' I said. 'What's goin' on?'

He shrugged and said, 'The usual.'

I sat opposite him.

'Can we talk here?' I asked.

'Nope.'

'Have they charged you?'

'Nope.'

'Is there anything you can tell me here and now?'

'Yeah,' he said, 'I didn't kill anybody.'

'Who got killed?'

'Some guy.'

'You don't know him?'

'Never met him,' Jerry said, 'never saw him before. They can't pin this on me. No motive.'

'So what do we do now, big guy?'

'We wait,' Jerry said. 'They gotta let me outta here sometime.'

'Entratter is sending a lawyer,' I said, 'so it may be sooner than you think.' I reached across the table and patted his arm. 'Sit tight.'

'I'm an expert, Mr G.'

I nodded, stood up and left the room. Hargrove was waiting outside.

'Well?'

'I got nothin',' I said, figuring he had heard the whole conversation, anyway. 'Except that he says he didn't kill anyone.'

'Yeah,' he said.

'Jack Entratter is sending a lawyer,' I told him. 'I'll wait around for him.'

'Then you better come to the squad room.'

He led the way to a room full of desks and, consequently, filled with cops.

'That's my partner,' he said, pointing to a smallish man sitting behind one of the desks. He had wispy blond hair that was thinning, making him look older than his mid-thirties, which was probably what he was. 'Detective Martin.' He looked at me. 'No relation to Dino. Henry, this is Eddie Gianelli.'

Martin nodded to me. 'I've heard about you.'

'Nothin' good, I'm sure,' I said. 'What'd you do to get stuck with Hargrove?'

'Just got lucky.'

'Another new partner, Hargrove?' I asked, as he sat behind his own desk. 'You go through partners like I go through...'

'...laws?'

'I don't break the law,'

'Naw,' Hargrove said, 'you just bend 'em right up to the breaking point.'

I declined to comment on that.

'Henry, Mr Gianelli says his boss, Jack Entratter, is sending a lawyer to get Jerry Epstein out.'

Henry Martin was sitting back in his chair with his head supported by his right hand against his cheek.

'We don't have anything on him, Hargrove,' he said. 'We could let him go before the lawyer gets here.'

'Not a chance,' Hargrove said. 'Let 'im sweat.'

'You've dealt with Jerry before, Hargrove,' I said. 'You really think he's sweating?'

'I don't care,' Hargrove said. 'He's been in Vegas what, half a day? And already I've got a body, with him on the scene.'

'Who got killed?' I asked.

Hargrove didn't answer, so I looked at Martin. He took a notebook from his pocket.

'William Reynolds,' he said, 'male, white, thirty, five-foot ten, one sixty, all according to his driver's license. Also according to his license, resides in Los Angeles.'

'So what was he doing here?' I asked.

'We don't know,' Martin said, closing the book. 'Gambling?'

'How did he die?'

'Shot,' Hargrove said.

'With what?'

'A gun,' he said.

'I assumed that much,' I said. 'What caliber?'

'Thirty-eight,' he said, 'and before you say anything else, I know where you're going. Your buddy doesn't have a gun on him, and when he does it's a forty-five.'

'You're a mind-reader,' I said. 'You'd think that would make you a good detective, but...'

That made Martin grin, but he hid it behind

89

his hand. I figured Hargrove had another partner who didn't like him much.

'Then why are you holding him?' I asked.

'Like I said,' Hargrove said. 'He was there.'

'Did you find him with the body?'

'No,' Martin said. 'He was outside the building.'

'Why was he even grabbed?'

'This was an odd one,' Martin said. 'The uniforms said when they rolled up on the scene he stepped up and put his hands behind his head.'

'He gave up?'

'Yup.'

'Did he say anything?'

'No.'

'Where's the victim now?'

'The morgue.'

'Can I have a look?'

Martin looked at Hargrove.

'Yeah, sure,' he said. 'I'll call ahead and leave your name.'

'If you recognize him you'll let us know, right?' Martin asked.

'Of course.'

'Yeah,' Hargrove said, 'sure.' His phone rang at that moment. He picked it up, said, 'Hargrove,' listened, then said, 'Yes, all right, send him back.' He hung up and looked at Martin. 'Epstein's lawyer is here.'

Martin nodded and stood up. 'I'll get him ready.' He looked at me. 'Nice to meet you.'

'Sure,' I said, 'same here.'

NINETEEN

The lawyer sent by Jack Entratter – Horace Daniels – walked Jerry and I out of the police station. The man was not only dwarfed by Jerry, but by me, as well. We were both able to look down at the bald spot on top of his head, barely covered by a comb-over.

'Mr Entratter wanted me to ask you boys not to kill anybody else this week,' Daniels said.

'Mr G. ain't killed nobody this week or any other week,' Jerry said.

'It's OK, Jerry,' I said, 'Jack's just being funny. Horace, just tell Jack everything's under control.'

Horace adjusted his wire-framed glasses on his little button nose and said, 'I hope so.'

He walked down the street to a waiting limo.

'I'm sorry, Mr G.—' Jerry started.

'I don't know what you think you have to be sorry for, big guy,' I said, 'but let's get in the Caddy and you can tell me about it.'

As we drove I asked, 'What's Reynolds got to do with Penny, Jerry?'

'I don't know, Mr G.,' he said. 'All I know is

I followed her there. She went inside. Before I could do anything she come running out, right into me. I ain't sure she recognized me, but she kept sayin' she didn't do it.'

'Then what?'

'I heard the sirens,' he said. 'Somebody musta called it in. The police cars pulled into the block, so I told her to go. When the patrol cars pulled up I did what I could to buy her some time.'

'You surrendered?'

'I put my hands on my head and waited,' Jerry said. 'I didn't say a word.'

'That's what probably saved you,' I said. 'All they had you for was being outside.'

'And Penny got away.'

'OK,' I said. 'Let's go and find Penny and discover who the fuck William Reynolds was.'

'Billy Reynolds is – was – an old boyfriend who showed up unexpectedly,' Penny said.

Penny had gone right home when Jerry gave her the time to escape, and stayed there. When she opened the door and saw us standing there she fell into my arms, saying, 'Oh, Eddie, I'm so sorry.'

After we went inside she apologized profusely to Jerry, and thanked him at the same time.

'OK Penny,' I said, 'why don't you tell us who this dead guy was?'

That's when she said, 'Billy Reynolds is –

was – an old boyfriend...'

'Showed up when?' I asked.

'A couple of weeks ago.'

'So you've been seeing him since then?'

'No, no,' she said, 'that's not it.' Penny was wearing a drawstring top and pulled it tightly around her slender frame. She shook her head so that her black ponytail kept bouncing up and down. 'I wasn't seeing him at all. I mean, not like that.'

'Then how?'

'He was forcing me to see him.'

'Forcing you how? And why didn't you just tell Danny about it?'

'You know Danny, Eddie,' she said. 'If I told him that Billy was blackmailing me, he would have killed him.'

'Blackmail?' I asked. 'What did he have to blackmail you with?'

She chewed her bottom lips, dug her hands into her pockets.

'I can't say, Eddie,' she replied, 'but if I had told Danny ... he would have killed Billy, for sure.'

'Well,' I said, 'somebody killed Billy, anyway. What happened when you went into that house?'

'Nothing,' she said. 'I found him and I ran. That's when I bumped into Jerry.' She looked at Jerry. 'And he saved me.'

'For now,' I said.

'What do you mean?'

'They let Jerry go because he has no motive to want to kill Billy Reynolds,' I said. 'He doesn't even know the guy. That means they're gonna be looking for somebody – somebody who lives in Vegas – who does know him.'

She bit her bottom lip again – chewed it, actually.

'When they check into this guy's background, are they gonna come up with you, Penny?'

She turned abruptly and walked away from us, pacing around her living room.

'Penny?'

She looked at me, her brow knitted, her eyes filling with tears.

'Come on, Penny,' I said. 'I can't help you if you don't tell me what's going on. When the police check into Billy Reynolds' background, are they going to come up with you?'

She stopped pacing and faced both of us, her hands still deep into her pockets.

'If they check up on him,' she said, 'they're gonna find out that we were arrested together – twice.'

TWENTY

'Arrested?' I asked.

'Some of my best friends' been arrested,' Jerry said to her. 'Ain't no shame in that.'

'There's shame in what I was arrested for,' she said.

'Was it murder?' Jerry asked.

'What? No!'

'Then there ain't no shame, miss.'

'Penny,' I said, 'for us to understand, you've got to tell us the whole story.'

She rolled her eyes, fought back the tears.

'Starting with why you were arrested.'

She closed her eyes, which caused a large tear to slip from both. They quickly trickled down her face and dripped off her chin.

'Can we sit down?' she asked, sounding exhausted.

'Of course,' I said. We'd been standing right there in the middle of her living room since we entered.

'Do you want somethin' to drink?' Jerry asked.

She sat on the sofa and touched her forehead.

'Water, I guess.'

'I could make you some tea,' he said. 'Do you have tea?'

'Yes, I have some.'

'Would you like a cup?'

She took a deep breath and let it out. 'That would be nice, Jerry.'

Her place had a kitchenette rather than a kitchen, so Jerry was able to make her the tea and still listen to her story.

'Penny?' I prodded her gently.

She took another deep breath, one that made her shoulders rise all the way up and then down again.

'I was seventeen,' she said, 'and homeless. And I met Billy. He was older – maybe twenty-five at the time.' She stopped. 'To make a long story short, he convinced me to do some things I didn't want to do. When we got arrested for stealing, I should have left him, but I couldn't. I still had nothing of my own. So I stayed. Then I got arrested for ... soliciting.' She lowered her head, and her shoulders slumped. She was totally humiliated.

'All right,' I said, 'it goes without saying that you were not actually soliciting,' I said. 'You did not actually do any hooking ... did you?'

Her head came up and she said, 'I didn't, I swear, Eddie!'

'I believe you, Penny,' I said. 'Danny would believe you, too.'

'I know that,' she said. 'Danny would never

96

think badly of me.'

'But you still didn't want to tell Danny about it.'

'No,' she said. 'He would have killed Billy for sure.'

I paused when I saw Jerry coming over with her tea. The delicate cup and saucer looked incongruous in Jerry's huge hands.

'Here ya go,' he said, setting it down on the coffee table in front of her. 'You want some sugar or milk?'

'Just sugar.'

He ran to the counter and came back with a sugar bowl. I noticed he had not made a cup for himself, or me.

'Thanks, Jerry.'

There were two armchairs that matched the sofa. I was in one, and Jerry settled his bulk into the other.

She sipped the tea and set it down.

'Is that OK?' Jerry asked.

'It's wonderful,' she said, 'thank you.'

'Penny.'

She looked at me.

'What's been going on since Billy showed up in Vegas?' I asked.

'I've been fending him off,' she said. 'When I ran into him on the street I thought it was a coincidence.'

'How long since you had seen him?'

'Oh ... must be ten years.'

'What happened?'

'He told me he had changed, gone legit. But his fortunes still hadn't changed. He was broke.'

'Did he ask you for money?'

'Not that first time, but later he called me and asked me to meet him. He was nervous, edgy, and asked me for money.'

'How much?'

'Five thousand.'

'But you didn't give it to him.'

'I didn't have five thousand dollars, Eddie,' she explained.

'But you gave him something, right?'

She looked down, ashamed again.

'Yes.'

'How much.'

'Twelve hundred,' she said. 'It was all I had in the bank.'

'Why did you empty your bank account?'

'I thought he would go away.'

'Oh, Penny,' Jerry said.

We both looked at him. I'd never heard that soft tone of voice from the big guy before. I can't even describe it, but it made me look at him.

'Givin' him anythin' just made sure he'd come back,' Jerry said.

'I know that now, Jerry.'

'Why didn't you just go to Mr G.?' he asked. 'He woulda helped you.'

She looked at me. 'I knew you'd help me, but ... I didn't want you to think badly of me, either.'

'So Billy came back for more?'

'And I told him I didn't have more, but he didn't believe me,' she said. 'He didn't want to believe me.'

'So he kept insisting.'

'Yes.'

'And what did you decide to do?'

'I thought I could get a loan,' she said, 'but it would only be one time.'

'And did he agree to that?'

'That's what I was meeting him about,' she said, 'only he was dead when I got there.'

'Did he say anything to you about somebody threatening him?'

'No,' she said. 'He told me he'd gone straight.'

'But you didn't really believe him, did you?' Jerry asked.

'No.'

'So are you surprised that somebody killed him?' I asked.

'Kind of,' she said. 'Everything he's ever been into has been petty, nothing to get killed over.'

'Well,' I said, 'somebody thought it was bad enough to kill him.'

'How do we find out who?' she asked.

'Why do we have to?' I asked. 'I mean, it's up to the cops, and unless they decide that you're a suspect, we can just sit tight. If we start asking questions now we might attract attention.'

'Mr G.,' Jerry said, 'they're gonna find her name in this guy's known associates file.'

'You're probably right, Jerry,' I said, 'but I still say let's wait and see. There's always the possibility that Penny won't have to deal with the police.'

Jerry gave me a look that clearly asked what I was smoking, but I figured Penny deserved the chance to stay out of the whole thing.

'What about Danny?' Penny asked.

'What about him?' I asked.

'Does he have to know?'

'I think that's up to you, Penny.'

'But ... what will you tell him?'

She still didn't know that Danny had asked me to check up on her, *and* she still hadn't asked why Jerry was where he was when she ran into him. That was good, because I hadn't had time to think up an answer for her. But she was going to come up with that question sooner or later.

'I'm not gonna tell him anything,' I said. 'Like I said, it's up to you.'

TWENTY-ONE

But I had to tell Danny something, didn't I?

Jerry and I left Penny's apartment, assured by her that she was not leaving.

'But I'll be at work tomorrow,' she added.

'That's fine,' I said.

'If you talk to Danny will you let me know, Eddie? I don't want any surprises.'

'I will,' I promised.

Outside Jerry asked, 'What are you gonna tell the Dick?'

'I don't know yet.'

'You gotta tell him the truth, right?' Jerry asked. 'I mean, he's your friend and he asked you to check up on his girl.'

We reached the Caddy and he got behind the wheel. I walked around and got in.

'Penny's my friend, too.'

'Yeah, but,' Jerry said, 'he's really your friend, right? From when you was kids in Brooklyn? That's gotta mean more, right?'

'Why? Because we were kids? Or because it was in Brooklyn?'

'Well ... both.' He started the car. 'Where to?'

'The Sands,' I said. 'Time to get you settled in your suite. Give you a chance to breathe. Know the way?'

'I think so.'

We pulled away from the curb and he handled the big Caddy with a sure hand.

'She's right, ain't she?' Jerry asked.

'About what?'

'The Dick,' he said. 'He woulda killed the guy.'

'Probably.'

'Maybe...' he started, then stopped.

'Maybe what?'

'I was thinkin',' he said, 'maybe he did find out, and maybe he did kill 'im.'

'If I thought that,' I said, 'then I'd have to look into it, wouldn't I?'

'Well, Mr G.,' he said. 'We'd have to look into it. I'm in this, too. After all, I was there.'

'Right, you were.'

We drove in silence and then he asked the other question that was on his mind.

'Mr G.?'

'Yeah?'

'What if she *did* do it?'

'Just keep drivin'.'

TWENTY-TWO

It was late when we got to the Sands – late, that is, for anyplace but Vegas. I took Jerry directly up to his suite.

'Your suitcase is in the bedroom,' I said. 'Do you want to turn in?'

'No,' he said, 'I want somethin' to eat. Gettin' grilled makes me hungry.' He had no idea he'd made a joke.

'OK,' I said. 'We can get something downstairs.'

'I wanna take a shower and change first.'

'Take your time,' I said. 'I'll make a call.'

'To the Dick?'

'Yeah.'

'Know what you're gonna tell 'im yet?'

'No.'

'Good luck.'

He went into the bedroom and in moments I heard the shower running. I sat on the sofa, moved the phone from the end table to the coffee table, and dialed Danny's number.

'Eddie,' he said when he realized it was me, 'you got somethin' for me?'

'I've got some things,' I said, 'but I don't

103

know how much to tell you.'

'What?' he said. 'Why wouldn't you tell me everything you've found out, Eddie?'

'I guess I should,' I said, 'but not right now, Danny. Let's have breakfast tomorrow.'

'Did something happen?' he asked. 'Is Penny OK?'

'Penny's fine,' I said.

'Then what's goin' on?'

'Danny—'

'Never mind breakfast,' he said. 'I'm comin' over there – as soon as you tell me where you are. Where are you? The Sands?'

'Yeah,' I said. 'OK, look, Jerry and I will be in the Garden Room. Meet us there.'

'OK,' he said. 'I'm on my way.'

'See you soon.'

I hung up and jumped when Jerry came into the room.

'That was a quick shower,' I said.

'That's what I said it was gonna be, Mr G.,' he said. 'Who you gonna see soon?'

'Danny,' I said. 'He's gonna meet us downstairs.'

'You gonna tell him now?'

'I couldn't put him off,' I said, 'and you're right. He deserves to know everything.'

'I like bein' right.'

'Yeah, well,' I said, 'don't make a habit of it. You ready?'

'Ready and hungry.'

'Yeah,' I said, surprising myself, 'me, too.'

TWENTY-THREE

Jerry and I had plates in front of us when Danny showed up.

'I'll have the same,' he told the waitress, as he took a chair at the table. Sitting in a booth with Jerry was just too confining. I didn't have much of a choice at the Horseshoe, but the Garden Room had tables as well as booths.

He flipped over the cup on the table in front of him and poured some coffee from the pot next to it.

'OK, guys,' he said, 'what's up?'

'Danny,' I said, 'Penny's OK, but she could end up in trouble.'

'What kind of trouble?' he asked. 'Was she seein' somebody?'

'There was an old boyfriend,' I said, 'but she wasn't seein' him. Not the way you think.'

'Then what?' he asked. 'In what way was she seein' him? Who is he?'

'OK,' I said, 'I know this'll be hard for you, but just relax and listen.'

I explained about Penny's old boyfriend showing up, and the demands he was making on her. Then I told him about Jerry following her, and about the boyfriend being found dead. Finally, Jerry's arrest while Penny had gone home and stayed there. During that time the waitress brought Danny his food. Jerry attacked, I picked and Danny just kind of played with his.

'I'm sorry you got nabbed, big guy,' he said, 'but thanks for coverin' for her.'

'Forget it,' Jerry said. 'They had nothin' on me.'

'OK,' Danny said to me. 'I listened. Why didn't she come to me?'

'She said if she told you about Reynolds you would've killed him.'

'I probably would've,' he said. 'Wait, does she think that I—'

'No, she doesn't think that.'

'Who do the police think did it? Besides Jerry, I mean?'

'The police don't know about Penny yet – but they will.'

'How?'

Jerry and I exchanged a glance.

'No point keepin' anything from me now.'

'Yeah, well, this is something Penny might want to tell you herself.'

'But will she?' he asked. 'Come on, Eddie. I know she probably made you promise but we go back a long way.'

'Brooklyn,' Jerry said.

'Yeah,' Danny said, 'Brooklyn.'

'OK,' I said. I told him about Penny's priors and the likelihood that the cops would find her by going through Reynolds' known associates list.

'Jesus,' he said, 'you think you know somebody...'

'She was just a kid,' Jerry said.

'Oh, I know that,' Danny said. 'I'm not gonna hold it against her. I just thought it was something I shoulda known already.'

'She was afraid,' I said.

'Yeah, I know,' Danny said. 'There's a lot of that goin' around. Well, I guess I better go and see her.'

'Danny—'

'Eddie, don't worry,' he said, standing up. 'I'll go easy. I just want her to know ... well, there are just things I want her to know.'

'Are you sure I shouldn't come along?'

'Positive,' Danny said. 'You guys have done enough, and I appreciate it. I'll call you.' He looked at Jerry. 'Take it easy, Gunsel.'

'You too, Shamus.'

He walked out of the Garden Room with Jerry and I watching him go.

'Think we did the right thing, lettin' him go alone?' he asked.

'They have a special relationship,' I said. 'It'll be OK.'

Jerry had finished his food. He pulled Danny's unfinished plate over and started in on it. I realized I was hungry and started in on mine in earnest.

'What'd he mean?'

'About what?'

'That thing about everybody bein' afraid. What's he afraid of?'

'Oh, that,' I said, chewing. 'I think he's afraid of letting Penny know how he really feels about her.'

'Don't he know she's crazy about him?' he asked. 'Anybody can see that.'

'Yeah, well,' I said, 'Danny's not anybody.'

'Well, I hope they talk to each other tonight,' Jerry said.

'So do I, big fella,' I said, 'so do I.'

'So what do we do now?' Jerry asked.

'Oh, I didn't tell you,' I said. 'Elvis is getting in tomorrow.'

'That's great, Mr G., but since you don't need me no more for this thing with Penny maybe ya wanna ship me back to Brooklyn?'

'You came all this way, Jerry,' I said. 'You should at least get to meet Elvis ... if you want to, that is.'

'Well, sure,' he said. 'Who don't wanna meet Elvis, huh?'

'OK then,' I said, 'you can come with me tomorrow when I go to the Riviera.'

'Breakfast first?' he asked.

I laughed and said, 'Yeah, of course, break-fast first.'

TWENTY-FOUR

Elvis' scheduled check-in time was ten a.m. I gave him time to settle in and showed up at the Riviera at eleven, with Jerry in tow.

The front of the hotel was already mobbed with fans who had somehow gotten word of Elvis' arrival. We drove around the back. There was a crowd there, too, but not as many. Still, we had to fight our way through to get inside. There were security men on the door holding the crowd out. Luckily, one of them knew me from the Sands and allowed us to enter, which raised the ire of the crowd.

'Must be nice to have people know you like that,' Jerry said.

'It has its moments,' I admitted.

I presented myself at the front desk and announced that I was there to see Elvis Presley.

'Eddie Gianelli.'

The clerk was a young guy who didn't recognize my name. He must have been new.

'Yes, sir,' he said, 'I have you on the approved visitor list.' He looked up at Jerry. 'And you, sir?'

'He's with me.'

'That may be, sir, but I can't allow him to go up unless he's on the list.'

'Well,' I said, 'call the room and ask Mr Presley.'

'I can't disturb—'

'Look,' I said, 'I'm expected, and I'm not going up without my friend. Now, do you want to tell Mr Presley or his people that you would not let me up?'

'Well, no sir, but—'

'Call ... or call Tommy.'

'Tommy?'

'Tommy Harper? The concierge here?'

'You're friends with Mr Harper?'

'Very good friends.'

'Just a minute, sir.'

He picked up the phone and called Tommy, grateful for an alternative to having to call Elvis' suite.

'Yes, sir,' I heard him say, 'he says he's here to see Elvis and he's a friend of yours. Uh-huh, Eddie Gianelli. Yes, sir. Thank you.'

He hung up and looked at us.

'Mr Harper will be right with you.'

'Thank you.'

We stepped away from the desk to wait.

'What an idiot,' Jerry said. 'He don't know who you are.'

'Lots of people don't know who I am, Jerry.'

'Naw, that ain't true, Mr G.,' Jerry said. 'Only the idiots.'

110

Tommy appeared in moments, walking across the lobby with purposeful strides. His red hair looked redder than ever, and he had that 'what, me worry?' Alfred E. Neuman look on his face.

'Geez...' Jerry said.

'I know.'

'He looks just like that *Mad* magazine guy.'

'I know.'

'Geez...'

I wondered how he'd look in twenty years or so, when he went grey – or bald?

'Eddie, what the hell...?' Tommy started.

'This is legit, Tommy,' I said. 'Elvis is waiting for me.'

'Yeah, but who's this guy?'

'Tommy, meet Jerry Epstein,' I said, 'a friend of mine from Brooklyn.'

'Brooklyn?'

Tommy was of the opinion that everybody from Brooklyn was a gangster. Looking at Jerry did nothing to disabuse him of that belief.

'Yeah, hello.'

'Hi.'

Tommy leaned in and whispered, 'You wanna take him up with you?'

'I do.'

'But—'

'I think you'll find that any friend of mine is a friend of Elvis',' I said. 'Call him and ask.'

'Call Elvis?'

'Yeah.'

'I'm supposed to wait until he calls me.'

'OK, look,' I said, 'I'll go to a house phone and call him myself.'

'Whataya gonna tell 'im?'

'Don't worry,' I said, 'I won't tell him that you and your clerk gave me a hard time. I'll just tell him I'm here and I want to bring Jerry up with me. OK?'

'Yeah, yeah, OK,' Tommy said. 'That sounds good. The house phones are over here.'

'I know where the house phones are, Tommy,' I said, but he walked us over to them, anyway.

I picked up the receiver and asked to be connected to Elvis Presley's room.

'Sir,' the operator said, 'I'm only supposed to put through people who are on the approved list.'

'I'm on the list,' I assured her. 'Eddie Gianelli.'

'Mr Gianelli,' she said, as if she recognized my name, 'yes, sir, I'll put you through.'

'Thank you.'

The phone rang and after three of them it was picked up and a morose voice said, 'Hello.' I recognized it right away.

'Hey Red, Eddie Gianelli here.'

'Yeah?'

'I'm, uh, downstairs, trying to get up.'

'So? Your name's on the list.'

'I know, but I've got a friend with me.'

'What for?'

'He's going to help me.'

'With what?'

'Red,' I said, 'would you do me a favor and ask Elvis if I can bring him up with me?'

'Does he want an autograph?'

'He doesn't.'

Red hesitated. Maybe he was shocked.

'Hold on.'

He muffled the receiver, probably with his hand, and called out to someone, presumably Elvis.

'Yeah okay,' he said, when he came back on, 'just come to the top floor.'

'What room?'

'Like I said,' Red answered, 'the top floor.'

I hung up and said to Jerry and Tommy Harper, 'It's OK.'

'What room?' Jerry asked.

TWENTY-FIVE

'The whole top floor?' Jerry said again, as we went up in the elevator.

'Yep.'

'Now that's money,' Jerry said.

'Serious juice,' I agreed.

The elevator door opened and Red West was standing there with his crew cut intact. He immediately looked Jerry up and down and while he may not have wanted it to show, I could see that he was impressed.

'This way,' he said. 'E's waitin'.'

I followed Red down the hallway, with Jerry bringing up the rear. Elvis had obviously taken over the Presidential Suite, which we entered, the door having been left ajar.

'...tell 'em to get it up here fast,' I heard Elvis saying to somebody.

We entered the suite and I saw Elvis seated on a sofa, speaking into the phone.

'There you are,' he said to Red. He held the phone out to him. 'We need a lot more Pepsi. A lot more.'

Red took the phone and said, 'I'll take care

of it.'

'Eddie!' Elvis said. 'I'm glad to see you. Who's your big friend?'

'Elvis, this is Jerry Epstein,' I said. 'Jerry, meet Elvis Presley.'

'Pleasure to meetcha,' Jerry said, putting out his hand.

'Wow,' Elvis said, 'you're a big boy.' He shook Jerry's hand. 'What a grip. You know karate?'

'No,' Jerry said.

'Too bad,' Elvis said. 'I'd love to work out with you.'

'Whataya mean, like, spar?'

'Yes, spar, that's what I mean.'

'We could spar,' Jerry said.

'Really?' Elvis asked. 'I'm a black belt, you know.'

Jerry grinned and said, 'I don't need no belt.'

'Whoa!' Elvis said. He turned to Red, who was hanging up the phone. 'Red, we got us a live one.'

'Yeah,' Red said.

'That Pepsi comin' up?' Elvis asked.

'Yeah, E,' he said. 'It's on the way.'

'It shoulda been here when we checked in.'

'I'll tell 'em.'

Elvis turned his attention back to us.

'What's on your agenda, Eddie?' he asked.

'I thought you might want to see the sights.'

'I do, but first I got a rehearsal this afternoon. How about tonight we go someplace to eat?'

115

'Suits me.'

'Bring Jerry, too,' Elvis said.

'Thanks,' Jerry said.

'Where are you from, Jerry?' Elvis asked.

'Brooklyn,' Jerry said, 'just like Mr G.'

'You guys be back here at eight tonight and we'll do it. Red, make sure Jerry's name is on the list, hear?'

'I hear, E.'

Elvis shook hands with both of us again.

'Where are the rest of the guys?' I asked.

'They got other rooms on this floor.'

'Will they be with us tonight?' I asked. 'Just so I know.'

'Oh yeah,' Elvis said, 'we're all goin' out to eat. Oh, Ann-Margret will be with us, too.'

'Ann-Margret?' Jerry asked.

Elvis looked at Jerry with a big grin on his face.

'I'll introduce you,' he promised. 'She likes big guys.'

'That'd be great,' Jerry said. 'I really like her.'

'She's a good girl,' Elvis said. 'And wait til you see her in this movie. What a talent. Red! Take them back to the elevator, will ya? I'll see you boys tonight.'

'We'll see you,' I said, and followed Red out of the room.

Red stopped right in front of it, but didn't press the button.

'You've got to press the button for it to work'

I said.

He turned his head, looked past me at Jerry.

'E wants to spar with you.'

'I know,' Jerry said. 'That's fine with me.'

'He's got a black belt,' Red said, 'but you strike me as the kinda guy that don't mean nothin' to.'

'I fight for real,' Jerry told him, 'not for belts.'

'I figured that,' Red said. 'I wouldn't take it too kindly if Elvis got hurt. You understand?'

'I understand,' Jerry said. 'I don't intend to hurt him.'

'Good,' Red said, ''cause if you do, you'll have to deal with me.'

Red wasn't as big as Jerry, but I thought it would be an interesting fight.

Jerry just stared at him.

TWENTY-SIX

In the Riviera lobby Jerry said, 'Who was he tryin' ta kid?'

'Red? He doesn't like anybody except Elvis and maybe Elvis' friends. Oh, and his cousin, Sonny.'

'He should watch how he treats strangers,' Jerry said. 'Somebody might get the wrong idea.'

'You *can* get the wrong idea about Red.'

We walked through the casino and out into the sun.

'So now we have time,' Jerry said. 'What do we do with it?'

'We could check with Danny and Penny, see how they're doing,' I said.

'Get somethin' to eat?'

'Eventually,' I said, 'like ... lunch?'

'I was just thinkin' of a snack.'

'Jerry,' I said, 'you're always thinking about a snack.'

'Mr G.,' he said, 'you say that like it's a bad thing.'

We drove to Fremont Street, parked around the corner from Danny's office and walked to the front door. It was locked. I had a key, but I tried ringing the bell.

'Nobody home,' Jerry said.

I held up the key.

'Shall we?'

'He gave it to you, didn't he?'

I unlocked the door and we went up the stairs. Once again I knocked, and when no one opened the door I used the second key.

The office was much the way I had left it last time. It didn't seem that anyone had been back.

I walked to Penny's desk and picked up her phone.

'Who you callin'?' Jerry asked.

'First Danny's place, then Penny's,' I said. 'They've got to be at one of them.'

But both phones rang with no answer.

'So maybe they're out getting somethin' to eat,' Jerry suggested. 'Or maybe they're doin' ... somethin'. You know, they're too busy to answer the phone?'

'That would be a good answer,' I said. 'OK, so then we wait for them to contact us. What do we do in the meantime?'

He gave me a meaningful look.

'OK, OK,' I said. 'We'll walk over to the Horseshoe, get you a snack, and do some thinking. I need to take Elvis and his crew someplace to eat, tonight.'

'Well,' Jerry said, 'I'm more worried about

119

eating now.'

'I can always count on you, Jerry,' I said.

'That's right, Mr G.,' he said. 'You can.'

We were talking about two different things, but both were true.

We slid into a booth at the Horseshoe's coffee shop. It wasn't so bad with Jerry on the other side. It was only when you tried to sit on the same side of a booth with Jerry that problems arose.

'Whataya have?' the bored looking waitress asked. 'Hey, I remember you.' She wasn't talking to me, she was talking to Jerry. 'You're the pancake man.' Suddenly, she wasn't bored. Her face lit up and I saw the young girl she had been twenty years ago, before her life had beat her down. Waitressing was supposed to be a transitional job. But when you held the same job for a long time, like she probably had, it was a rut.

'That's me,' Jerry said. 'I'll have a stack.'

'Just one?' she asked. 'We talk about you in here, you know. Nobody's ever eaten as many pancakes as you – and hey, you done it a few times, right?'

'Whenever I'm in town,' Jerry said. 'But right now we're just here for a snack.'

'A snack, huh?'

'Yep,' he said. 'One stack.'

She looked at me.

'Coffee.'

'That's all?' she asked, the bored look coming back.

'An order of French fries.'

'Comin' up.'

'How many friends does Elvis have, Mr G.?' Jerry asked. 'I mean, with him.'

'Well, there's Red, Sonny ... probably five, plus him, plus Ann-Margret...'

'...and you and me.'

'Right. So about nine.'

'What about a show?' Jerry asked. 'Some showgirls? Booze. Food. Always works with the people I deal with.'

'I'm thinkin' about something else,' I said. 'Elvis doesn't go to shows, he performs them. I'm thinkin' of takin' them to the Bootlegger, and then some gambling.'

'The Bootlegger. Been there, right?'

'Yeah,' I said, 'it's a favorite of Frank's.'

'What about Mr S. Will he wanna go, too?'

'I don't think Frank would want to hang around with Elvis' crew,' I said. 'Besides, he's going to stop in on one of Elvis' shows.'

'Well,' Jerry said, 'all I care about is, I'm gonna meet Ann-Margret.'

'You like her, huh?'

'Well, she ain't Marilyn or Miss Gardner,' Jerry said, 'but she's a cute kid.'

'Yeah, she is.'

'I seen her in *State Fair* and *Bye Bye Birdie*. I bet she's sexier in *Viva Las Vegas*. I bet she's gonna do lots of sexy parts.'

121

'I'll bet she is,' I agreed.

'Hey, are they gonna show *Viva Las Vegas*? You know, a preview?'

'I know they're here to promote it, but I don't think they're gonna show it. If they do I'll get you in, don't worry.'

'I never worry about you, Mr G.,' Jerry said. 'I know you always take care of me.'

Said the man who had saved my life more times than I could count.

TWENTY-SEVEN

We left the Horseshoe and drove back to the Sands, for want of something better to do. I figured I'd use a phone there to make some reservations for that night for Elvis and his guests.

As I entered, one of the bellmen came running over. He almost ran me down before he could stop.

'Eddie, Mr Entratter's been lookin' for you all morning,' he said.

'What's it about?'

'All he said was I was to grab you as soon as you came in and send you up. That was a couple of hours ago. I been lookin' out for you ever since.' He spoke quickly, without taking a breath.

'OK–' I looked at the name on his ID plate – 'Billy, thanks.' I turned and looked at Jerry. 'You want to come up with me?'

'Sure,' he said. 'I like Mr Entratter.'

'Let's go.'

We took the elevator to Jack Entratter's floor and walked to his office. His girl looked up as we entered, frowned twice as deeply as usual, probably due to Jerry's presence.

'He's been looking for you.'

'I heard.'

I suppose she was happy there was no more need for her to speak to me. I went into Jack's office, followed by Jerry.

'I heard you're lookin' for me, Jack.'

'What's goin' on?' Entratter demanded. 'What have you two been into now?'

'What do you mean?'

'A young lady named Penny has been callin' here every ten minutes for the past two hours lookin' for you or Jerry.'

'She had a problem we were helping her with.'

'When you're supposed to be takin' care of that Elvis thing?'

'Don't worry, Jack,' I promised, 'it won't get in the way.'

'I'm glad you think so,' he said. 'She wants you to meet her at the police station.'

'What for?'

'Apparently,' Jack said, 'your buddy the private eye has been arrested.'

'For what?'

'Murder.'

TWENTY-EIGHT

When we got to the station, Penny was waiting by the front desk.

'Oh, my God!' she said, running up to me. 'I've been calling everywhere looking for you.'

'We've been looking for you, too,' I said. 'We went to your office and called both of you at home.'

'They came for him this morning, just as we were opening the office.'

'Who was it?'

'Who else? Hargrove? He was so happy while he was putting the cuffs on Danny.'

'Who do they say Danny killed?'

'Eddie, it was Billy Reynolds.'

'What? How do they figure that?'

'I don't know,' she said. 'They won't even talk to me.'

'What about Danny's lawyer?'

'I called him,' she said. 'His secretary says he's in court. She'll give him the message and get him here as soon as possible. Eddie, Danny's been alone back there for hours!'

'OK,' I said, 'try to relax. Let me see what I

can find out. Jerry?'

I walked to the desk. Jerry wasn't quite sure what to do, but Penny solved that problem for him. She grabbed one of his big arms and held on.

'Help ya?' the sergeant at the desk asked.

'Eddie Gianelli to see Detective Hargrove.'

'I'll check and see if he has time for you,' the sergeant said. 'He's kinda busy.'

'Oh,' I said, 'I think he'll see me.' If just to rub Danny's arrest in my face.

The sergeant made a short call, then hung up, looking surprised.

'Someone will be right out,' he said.

'Thanks.'

The 'someone' was the dapper Detective Henry Martin, Hargrove's new partner.

'I'll take you back,' he said.

I turned to Penny and Jerry and said, 'Come on.'

'Not him,' Martin said, pointing, 'and not her. Just you.'

'It's OK, Eddie,' Penny said. 'Just go. Danny needs you.'

'Lead the way,' I told Martin, even though I was fairly sure I knew the way.

As I followed him down a familiar hall he asked, 'What'd you ever do to Hargrove, Mr Gianelli? He sure has it in for you and your friends.'

'I often wonder that same thing,' I said. 'I think he just doesn't like what I do for a living.'

126

'I don't think he's after you because you're a pit boss,' Martin said. 'It must be something else.'

'Well then, I guess it has something to do with who I work for.'

'The Sands?'

'Or Jack Entratter,' I said.

'Or maybe it's who Jack Entratter works for,' Martin said, 'because Hargrove really does have a hard-on for the mob.'

'Well, I'm not in the mob,' I said.

'But you have mob affiliations.'

'My affiliations are with the Sands,' I said. 'That's it.'

'Well,' Martin said, 'this is for you and him to resolve. I'm just along for the ride.'

'For how long?' I asked. 'Hargrove's partners don't usually stick around very long.'

'I do happen to have my eye on another situation,' he admitted.

We had reached the interview rooms and Martin said, 'Stay here.' He went into a room and came out with Hargrove.

'I've been waiting for you,' he said with an unfriendly smile. 'Come with me.'

He took me to another interview room with just a table and two chairs.

'Am I under arrest, too?' I asked.

'Of course not,' Hargrove said. 'This is just a place for us to talk. Have a seat.'

Just to keep it from feeling like I was under arrest I sat on the side he'd usually take. He didn't mind. He sat across from me.

'So what's goin' on, Hargrove?' I asked. 'First you try to pin this murder on Jerry, and now Danny? Who's next? Me?'

'No, not you, Eddie,' Hargrove said. 'But your buddy's girl, Penny O'Grady, might be next.'

'Penny? Why her?'

'Don't act innocent with me, Eddie,' he said. 'You knew when I had Jerry in here yesterday that the dead man was her old boyfriend.'

'No,' I said, 'actually, I didn't.'

He studied me for a moment, then said, 'You know what, Eddie? This is one of the few times I believe you.'

'Why don't you tell me what this is all about, detective? This murder only happened yesterday and already you've made two arrests.'

'I know how to do my job, Eddie,' Hargrove said. 'It didn't take us long to find Penny's connection to William Reynolds, our dead man.'

'Connection?'

'They were partners once,' Hargrove said. 'Boyfriend and girlfriend. Come on, don't tell me you don't know she's got a sheet.'

'I do know,' I said, 'but that was a long time ago. She was young.'

'That's what they all say,' he replied. 'As if being young forgives everything.'

'Some things.'

'Well, maybe not this,' Hargrove said. 'Once we had the girl's name it led us right to your

128

buddy the keyhole peeper. The rest was easy.'

'Why easy?'

'Because we canvassed the neighborhood where the murder took place and came up with Danny Bardini's description.'

'Lots of guys look like Danny.'

'Yeah, but lots of guys don't drive his car, with his license plate.'

'Somebody else could have been driving it.'

'Well, it hasn't been reported stolen,' Hargrove said. 'Reynolds was shot with a thirty-eight. Bardini carries a thirty-eight.'

'Has it been fired recently?'

'It has. We got it off of Bardini when we took him in. I should have a ballistics match soon.'

Damn.

'What about his lawyer?'

'I believe we're waiting for him. Not being sent by your boss, is he?'

'Danny has his own lawyer.'

'Good,' Hargrove said, 'then I won't have to deal with another goddamned mob lawyer.'

'Look, can I see him?'

'Sure,' Hargrove said, 'maybe you can get him to confess.'

'I'm sure he didn't do it.'

'Your loyalty is admirable. Come on. I'll give you fifteen minutes.'

'Very generous.'

'I'm a generous guy.'

We left the room, went down the hall to another door.

TWENTY-NINE

'In you go,' Hargrove said. 'Fifteen minutes.'

I opened the door and entered. It was a room like the one I'd just left, furnished with a table and two chairs. Danny sat at the table, looking disheveled, like he hadn't slept in hours. There were several empty coffee containers on the table, and an empty Milky Way wrapper.

'Crap,' he said, 'I thought it was my lawyer.'

'Nice to see you, too.'

'Have a seat,' Danny said. 'Sorry I can't offer you some refreshment.'

I pulled out the other chair and sat across from him.

'What's goin' on, Danny?'

'That's what I want to know,' he said. 'We went to work today and the cops were waitin' for us. I didn't know what the hell was going on until we got here and they told me I was under arrest for killin' William Reynolds.'

'Did you and Penny talk about Reynolds?'

'We did,' he said. 'Old boyfriend who took advantage of her, blah blah blah. What do I care? I only care about who she is now.'

'That's fine,' I said. 'Now tell me you've never seen Billy Reynolds in your life.'

He didn't say anything.

'Danny?'

'I can't say that, Eddie.'

'Oh Danny,' I said. 'You didn't tell me the whole story, did you?'

'No, buddy, I didn't,' he said. 'I'm really sorry, Eddie.'

'OK,' I said, 'let's talk about that later. Just tell me you didn't kill the guy.'

'I didn't kill the guy.'

I nodded. 'I believe you.'

'So now what?'

'So now I guess we have to wait for your lawyer,' I said. 'Look, I don't have much time. They say they got your description and your plate number, that you were in the area around the house.'

'I was,' he said, 'but I didn't kill him. I just wanted to talk to the guy, to convince him to leave Penny alone.'

'And did you talk to him?'

'I did.'

'Did you convince him of anything?'

'I didn't,' he said.

'What else?'

'I flattened him.'

'And?'

'That's it,' he said. 'He said Penny was gonna have to pay to get rid of him. I ... I told him there were easier ways, and I hit him. Just once.'

'And then?'

'And then I left.'

'What'd you mean when you said there were easier ways?'

'I was just trying to scare him, but the guy didn't scare.'

'OK, quick,' I said, 'tell me what you saw when you were there.'

'Not much,' Danny said. 'I've been thinkin' about it. I didn't see anyone else, didn't see any other cars. Not when I got there, and not when I left. As a witness, I'm fuckin' useless.'

'You can say that again.'

The door opened at that moment and cut off any retort he might have had.

'You're done,' Hargrove said.

'My lawyer here yet?' Danny asked.

'Not yet. But don't worry, you'll be the first to know.'

'Can I have another minute—' I started, but I knew the answer even before he cut me off.

'Not a chance,' Hargrove said. 'You're done. Let's go.'

'I'll see you later,' I said to Danny.

'My lawyer will get me out, Eddie,' he said. 'I didn't kill anybody. Take Penny home.'

'I'll have Jerry take her, and stay with her,' I said. 'I'll stick around until your lawyer gets here.'

'Thanks.'

'Hey, pit boss!' Hargrove snapped. 'Out!'

I left the room, followed by Hargrove, who slammed the door.

'He still singin' the same tune, huh?' he asked. 'He didn't do it?'

'That's because he didn't.'

'We'll see. Martin will take you back to the front.'

'Like I told Danny,' I said, 'I'll be around until his lawyer shows.'

'Suit yourself.'

Martin appeared at my elbow as if by magic and said, 'This way.'

Sneaky bastard.

THIRTY

'Is he all right?' Penny asked anxiously when I got back to the front.

'He's fine,' I said. 'He wants you to go home.'

'Eddie, I can't—'

'You have to, Penny,' I said. 'I'll stay. Don't make Danny worry about you while he's fighting to get out of here.' I turned to Jerry. 'Will you take her home in the Caddy?'

'Sure, Mr G.'

'And stay with her,' I said.

'How you gonna get back?' he asked. 'You got that Elvis thing—'

'I'll call you to come and get us when Danny gets out.'

'What about Elvis?'

'Don't worry about him,' I said. 'I'll take care of it.'

'Elvis?' Penny asked.

'Jerry will tell you on the way home,' I said. 'Go ahead, go.'

'Eddie...'

'Shoo!'

She pointed her finger at me and said, 'Call me!'

'I will.'

Jerry ushered her out of the building.

With Penny taken care of all I had to do was wait there for Danny's lawyer, who I had met only once or twice before, in passing, but who I would know on sight.

Jerry was right, though. I did have to deal with the Elvis thing. I still hadn't made a reservation, and I had to pick out a show to take them all to. But all of that depended on me – and Danny – getting out of the police station at a reasonable time.

I went across the street to a diner to get some coffee, then sat down on a bench in the lobby to wait for the lawyer.

I was starting to think I should call Elvis and make some excuse when the double doors opened and the lawyer came in. He must have gotten out of court early because it was only four p.m. He had a leather briefcase tucked beneath one arm.

'Mr Kaminsky?'

He looked at me, squinting as if he recognized me but couldn't place me. But he was hard to forget. Aaron Kaminsky was all of five foot four, about forty-five, wearing a blue suit that was several years old and several weeks past needing a cleaning. But Danny trusted him, said he was a great lawyer.

135

'Eddie Gianelli,' I said. 'Danny's friend from—'

'Sure, Eddie G.,' he said, triumphantly. 'Of course Kaminsky knows you. You wanna fill me in before I go inside? I don't want any surprises. Kaminsky hates surprises like I hate schmaltz.'

The thing I always notice about Aaron Kaminsky is that there's no telling when he will start referring to himself in the third person. It just makes him that much more of a character.

'That's what I'm here for.'

I gave him the rundown on everything I knew, holding nothing back.

'Is that it?' he asked. 'All of it?'

'All I know,' I assured him.

'OK,' he said, 'you're Danny's oldest friend, and you've got this whole town wired. So tell me what you think.'

'I think somebody killed Reynolds, and Hargrove is trying to pin it on Danny,' I said. 'He already tried to pin it on Jerry.' Identifying Jerry had been part of my original story, so he nodded.

'But Penny did have a relationship with this nudnik, right?'

'Right.'

'Years ago.'

'Right.'

'And she has a sheet from back then.'

'Right again.'

'OK, Bubula,' he said, 'I got it. Lemme go

136

get our friend out of the clink. You gonna wait here?'

'Yes.'

'Good.' He patted me on the arm. 'Don't worry. Kaminsky won't leave here without Danny.'

'Me, neither.'

So we bonded and then he was taken into the back to work his magic...

The next time I saw Kaminsky the lawyer was twenty-five minutes later, when he came walking out with Danny in tow. If possible, Kaminsky looked even more disheveled than Danny did.

'Hey, pal,' I said, giving Danny a hug. He smelled funky. 'You smell like the joint.'

'Thanks.' He turned to Kaminsky and hugged him. 'Thanks, Kaminsky.'

'Don't leave town, Bubula, or Kaminsky's ass is in a sling, eh?' He pointed his finger at Danny, then slapped him lightly on the cheek.

'You got it.'

Kaminsky left.

'He must be as good as you say,' I commented.

'He's the best. Come on, let's get out of here,' Danny said.

'Do you want me to call Jerry to come and get us?' I asked.

'Is he with Penny?'

'Yeah.'

'Nah, just leave him there,' Danny said. 'Let's get a cab.'

'OK.'

We left the station, caught a cab right out front that was letting off a weeping woman.

'Broad got robbed,' the driver said. 'Been snivelin' ever since. Where to, boys?'

'You're all heart,' Danny said, as we got into the back seat.

'Hey, when you've dropped off as many cryin' broads here as I have, you get like that, ya know?'

'Yeah,' Danny said, 'I know.' He gave the driver Penny's address, and off we went.

THIRTY-ONE

When Danny and I got to Penny's place she hugged him, and then made the same pronouncement I did.

'You stink,' she said. 'Take a shower.'

'Yes, ma'am.' He looked at us. 'You gonna be here when I get out?'

'We've got something to do,' I said.

'Eddie has to go to dinner with Elvis Presley,' Penny said.

'Really? Elvis?' Danny said, raising his eyebrows. 'Wasn't I supposed to be in on that?'

'Well, yeah,' I said, 'before you got arrested for murder.'

'Yeah, but now I'm out.'

'You're not going anywhere, Danny Bardini,' Penny said, firmly. 'We still have some talking to do.'

'And so do we,' I said, 'but we'll have to do ours tomorrow.'

'You go and enjoy your dinner, Eddie,' Penny told me. 'Don't worry about us.'

'I am worried,' I said, 'and I'll be back tomorrow. Whatever plan you come up with to deal with this thing, I want to be in on it.'

'OK,' Danny said, 'I want to thank both you guys for your help.'

'Don't mention it,' Jerry said.

'And don't hug me again,' I said, 'not until you take that shower.'

'I'm goin', I'm goin'.'

He disappeared into the bathroom, and Penny walked us to the door, sending us both off with a kiss on the cheek. Jerry blushed. I didn't.

We drove back to the Sands, where I found a phone and hurriedly made plans for an evening of fun and games with Elvis and the Memphis Mafia...

Like we planned, we took Elvis and his entourage to the Bootlegger, an Italian restaurant off the strip that Frank Sinatra had actually introduced me to. Aside from me, Jerry and Elvis there were Red and Sonny West, Billy Smith, Lamar Fike, Marty Lacker. Oh, and Ann-Margret. We were given a table for ten and were taken very good care of...

We ate family style, platters of food all over the table. Elvis ordered most of what was on the menu, so we started with salad and antipasto, then there were pasta, meatballs, chicken, prime rib, and veal dishes.

I sat on Elvis' right, Ann-Margret on his left. For some reason, he spent most of his time talking to me. Jerry sat to Ann-Margret's left, and she talked to him all night. He was in heaven. I knew that because every so often he threw a look my way and I could see it in his eyes.

'What else have you got planned for to-night?' Elvis asked me halfway through the meal.

'I've got tickets for a show at the Stardust ... the *Lido De Paris*.'

'Not a singer, I hope,' Elvis said.

'No,' I said, 'showgirls.'

'Good,' he said, 'the guys'll like that.'

'And you?'

'I'm gonna go back to the hotel while the boys go to the show. Then they'll wanna do some gambling.'

'And what will you do?'

'Watch some TV,' he said, 'order room service, plan my set lists.'

'And what's Ann going to do?' I asked.

'She's gonna go back to her hotel,' he said. 'She needs her beauty sleep.'

'So you're going to your room ... alone?'

'Unless you wanna come and hang out,' he said. 'I checked the listings. There's some good westerns on tonight.'

If I let him go to his room alone, there was no telling what kind of trouble he could get into. And the Colonel wanted me to keep him out of trouble.

'Well,' I said, 'I could come with you. You might be interested in what I was doing today.'

'What's that?'

141

I didn't know what I was getting into when I said, 'A friend of mine was arrested for murder. I was trying to help him.'

'What, whoa, whoa,' he said, turning his whole body toward me. 'Tell me more. In fact, tell me all about it.'

I told him just enough. But it wasn't enough. Not nearly.

After dinner the crew piled into a limo and headed for the Stardust. Since it didn't matter to me if they got into trouble I didn't send Jerry with them. Red hesitated, wanting to go back to the hotel with Elvis, who convinced him otherwise. Finally, the big guy got into the limo with the others.

'Hey, Jerry,' Elvis said, 'would you do me a big favor?'

'Whatever you want, Mr Presley.'

'Oh, hey, na, na, na, none of that "Mr" stuff. You call me Elvis.'

'OK...' Jerry said, but I knew that would never happen.

'Would you take Miss Margret back to her hotel in that big Caddy of yours?'

'Um, the Caddy is Mr G.'s, but sure ... if he says it's OK.'

Ann-Margret was standing off to one side, arms folded, looking beautiful in a simple blue sweater and brown skirt. Her red hair hung almost to her shoulders in soft waves. I noticed something I'd never seen on the big screen.

142

She had freckles.

'Sure, Jerry,' I said. 'Take Miss Margret back to her hotel, and then go on back to the Sands.'

'What are you gonna do, Mr G.?' Jerry asked.

I looked at Elvis and said, 'I guess I'm going back to Elvis' hotel to watch some TV.'

THIRTY-TWO

Elvis wanted the whole story.

'This is a real life murder case,' he said, when we got back to his room, 'with a private eye and everything. I wanna hear it all.'

'Well...' I said.

'I'm gonna order some more dessert from room service,' he said. 'You want somethin'?'

'Coffee,' I said, 'lots and lots of coffee.'

'Comin' up...'

He ordered several pots of coffee, brownies, banana pudding, ice cream – chocolate and vanilla – with shredded coconut and other toppings. From the bar he got a six pack of Pepsi.

We sat on the sofa with this repast spread out before us and I said, 'Are we gonna watch TV?'

'After you tell me the story of this murder,' he said. 'The whole story.'

'Well, Elvis,' I said, 'I don't know that I have the right to tell you all—'

'Eddie,' he said, 'I may be a country boy from Tupelo, but I ain't stupid.'

'I never thought you were.'

'Then don't you think I know why the Colonel wants you around me? To see that I don't get into trouble with my boys?'

'Uh...'

'To see that I don't give a butt load of money to some phoney preacher guy?'

'Well...'

'To see that I don't get into trouble any one of a dozen other ways I can find here in Sin City?'

'What are we doin' here, Elvis?'

He spread his hands out over the food on the coffee table and said, 'We're just two guys havin' dessert and talkin' about the events of the day.'

'Events of the day?'

'Yeah,' he said, picking up a brownie. 'Why don't we start with murder?'

I leaned forward, poured myself a cup of coffee, picked up a brownie and said, 'So, there's this guy named Reynolds...'

Elvis' attention – except for an occasional bite of brownie or spoon full of banana pudding – was absolute. I did keep some things back, things that were Danny and Penny's business only, and certain things about what Jerry actually did for a living. And the parts about my past dealings with Detective Hargrove. I mean, he didn't need to know *everything*.

When I was done he leaned back and said, 'Wow. This is better than a movie. And it's sure a dang sight better than any of my movies.'

145

'Some of your movies are pretty good,' I offered, but he ignored me.

'So what are you gonna do next?'

'Right now it's up to Danny and his lawyer,' I explained.

'You ain't gonna keep workin' the case?' he asked, eyes wide with surprise. Or maybe he was just disappointed in me.

'Elvis,' I said, 'I'm not a detective. I did what I could, but the rest is up to them.'

'But the gal came to you for help,' he said. 'And so did your buddy. And when your buddy's in trouble you got to do somethin' about it.'

Oh great, I thought, he thinks this is *The Maltese Falcon*.

'Elvis,' I said, 'I'm ready and willing to give Danny any help he needs. We've been friends for a long time. But he's the detective, and he has a lawyer. They're the professionals, not me.'

He popped a Pepsi can open, drained half of it and put it down on the table. He seemed to be thinking hard about something before he spoke again.

'Well, OK,' he said. 'How about watching one of those westerns?'

'Sure,' I said, 'right now I've got nothing better to do.'

In the morning I was going to have to call the Colonel – and probably Frank – and tell them that Elvis had scoped me out. Elvis was right, his good ol' boy surface did make people underestimate him.

'Let's get some popcorn,' he said, grabbing the phone and dialing room service. 'You like butter? I really like it with butter.'

'Sure, butter's fine.'

Jesus, I thought, I'm going to need Jerry's constitution just to keep up with him.

THIRTY-THREE

I watched two movies with Elvis and we didn't talk about the murder case again. He seemed to have forgotten about the whole thing, but I wasn't going to underestimate him again.

'I got to get some shut eye,' he said, after the second movie. 'There's a rehearsal in the morning, and a thing to do with Ann for the movie in the afternoon. You wanna come to one of those?'

'You know the Colonel sent me to watch you and you still want me around?' I asked.

'Well, sure, Eddie,' he said, slapping me on the shoulder. 'Dang, boy, I like you!'

'Well then ... yeah, I'd like to do the afternoon thing with you and Ann-Margret.'

'OK, then.' He walked me to the door. 'Meet me here at one and we'll go together.'

'What about the others?'

'Well, maybe Red,' he said. 'And, oh yeah, bring Jerry. I like that big guy, too. Sure would like to spar with him.'

'We can probably arrange that.'

'Good, good,' he said, opening the door

'Then I'll see you at one. 'night, Eddie.'

'Good night, Elvis.'

He closed the door, leaving me standing in the hall, wondering if I'd done the right thing in telling him about the murder.

But then I figured, what harm could it have done?

When I got back to the Sands I called Jerry's room. It was late everywhere but Vegas, and I figured he'd be up. I was right. He was awake, and he wanted to talk.

'Want me to come up?' I asked.

'Naw, let's meet in the coffee shop—'

'I can't eat another thing, Jerry,' I said. 'Meet me in the bar and we'll have a drink.'

'OK, Mr G.'

I was sitting at the bar in the Silver Queen Lounge when Jerry appeared. I had two beers waiting. He picked one up and gulped half. To him it was a sip, but to me it was a gulp.

'I gotta tell ya, Mr G., that Ann-Margret,' he said, excitedly, 'she's as sexy as Marilyn when you spend time with her that close up. When she gets a little older she's gonna be dangerous!'

'I can't disagree with you there,' I said.

'How'd it go with you and Mr Presley?'

'We ate, watched TV, and talked.'

'Talked about what?'

'Murder.'

'You told him about it?' he asked. 'How

149

much?'

'Most of it.'

'What'd he say?'

'He was interested, excited, but he seemed to think it was my duty to solve the thing. I mean, he gave me that *Maltese Falcon* speech.'

'I like that movie,' he said. 'You mean that speech Sam Spade gives about doin' something about your partner gettin' killed?'

'That's the one.'

'Well, the dick ain't dead and he ain't your partner, but I guess I could see why he'd think that. You guys been friends a long time.'

'Yeah, we have,' I said, 'but like I told Elvis, I'm not a detective, Jerry.'

'You got all the earmarks of a good private dick, Mr G.'

'Thanks, Jerry, but I have a job. As long as Danny's on the street, he and his lawyer can work on the murder.'

'Suit yerself, Mr G.,' he said. 'What are we doin' tomorrow?'

'Elvis has got a publicity thing in the afternoon. He invited us along.'

'With Miss Margret?'

'She'll be there.'

'Good.'

At that moment Frank walked into the room, looked around, spotted us and headed over. Jerry saw where I was looking and turned his head.

'Oh, I meant to tell you,' he said, 'Mr S. was

lookin' for ya, wanted me to call 'im as soon as I hears from you.'

'So you told him we were meeting here?'

He looked at me like he was a puppy and I had a rolled-up newspaper in my hand.

'Was that OK?'

'It was fine, Jerry,' I said. 'Just fine.'

THIRTY-FOUR

Frank was wearing a suit, nothing fancy, just a grey suit with a blue tie. Not something he'd wear on stage or out to dinner. He smiled broadly as he approached, and spread his arms out.

'Well, here's my boys,' he said, putting an arm around each of us. 'What'll you have? I'm buyin'.'

We had another beer each and he ordered a Martini.

'I heard Elvis got to town today,' he said to me. 'Everything all right?'

'Everything's fine, Frank,' I said. 'In fact, I just left him. He was going to bed.'

'That's great,' Frank said. 'He's a growin' boy, needs his sleep.'

'He's a good kid,' I said.

'That he is,' Frank said. 'I talked to Jack, though. He said you might be havin' some other problems? Somethin' that might take you away from the, uh, task at hand?'

I looked at Jerry.

'Jerry didn't tell me a thing,' Frank said,

152

quickly. 'In fact, Jack told me hardly anything. I think they were leavin' that up to you, Pally.'

I sighed, knowing I was going to have to tell the story – again.

'Have a seat, Frank...'

'I know Bardini,' Frank said.

'Yes,' I said, 'you've met him a few times.'

'He's no killer. At least, not in this sense.'

'I agree.'

'So how are you gonna help him and stay on Elvis?' Frank asked.

'I've done what I can for Danny, Frank,' I said. 'My focus is on Elvis.'

'Really?' Frank looked confused. 'I thought you guys were friends. Partners, almost. What was it Bogart said about partners?'

'That's what I said,' Jerry commented. *The Maltese Falcon.*'

'I love that movie,' Frank said.

'Me, too,' Jerry agreed.

'Hey, guys,' I said, 'I'm not a private dick. I'm not Danny's partner. And if he needs me, he'll call me.'

'Well,' Frank said, putting his empty Martini glass on the bar and getting to his feet, 'if you need any help with either thing, give me a call. In fact, Dino'll be here tomorrow. You helped us plenty of times. I know he'd want to help your buddy, too.'

'Thanks, Frank,' I said. 'I appreciate that.'

Frank waved and left.

'Wow,' Jerry said, 'Mr S and Dino workin' with you on a murder case!'

'I'm not working on a murder case, Jerry!' I said.

'No, I know, I know,' he said, 'but you never know ... ya know?'

Man, I would replay that comment later!

I decided to drive home and sleep in my own bed. I told Jerry I'd catch up with him in the morning, and that he should have breakfast without me.

When the phone rang I groped for it while trying to steal a look at the clock. Seven a.m. I'd been in bed exactly three hours.

'Yeah, wha—'

'Eddie? Eddie, it's Penny.' Her voice sounded panicked. 'They did it again, Eddie. They just came for Danny and arrested him. And this time they say they have proof!'

THIRTY-FIVE

I ran into Kaminsky on the front steps of the station, the same briefcase tucked under his arm. Penny said she would call him after we hung up. I wondered why she didn't call him first.

'What's going on, Mr Kaminsky?' I asked.

'I suspect I know what you know, Bubula,' he said. 'I've got to get inside to find out more. You want in?'

'How are you going to get me in?' I asked.

'From this point on,' he said, 'you're my investigator.' He took a dollar from his pocket and handed it to me.

'OK,' I said, pocketing the bill, 'boss.'

We went inside together.

Hargrove was incensed.

'What do you mean he's your investigator?' he demanded. 'That's bullshit!'

'He's working for me. Getting his time in so he can get his PI ticket,' Kaminsky said.

'You paid?' Hargrove demanded of me.

The one dollar bill was burning a hole in my

pocket as I said, 'I am.'

Hargrove looked over at Martin and said, 'OK, let 'em in.'

Martin took us down the hall from the bull pen to the interview rooms.

'Detective, would you like to tell me why you've dragged my client back in here less than twenty-four hours after you cut him loose?' Kaminsky asked.

'New evidence,' Martin said.

'What new evidence?'

We stopped in front of the door to the same interview room as before and Martin turned to face us.

'Hargrove would have my ass if he knew I told you,' he said.

'Then why tell us?' I asked.

'Maybe because he's a prick,' he said. 'We got the ballistics report back. The bullet in the victim matches your boy's gun. You better convince him to come clean.' He opened the door. 'Go ahead.'

We went into the room, found Danny sitting at the same table. He wasn't quite as disheveled as last time. In fact, he'd had a good night's sleep and a shower, but they must have pulled him out of bed because he looked as if he had dressed in a hurry.

'Well,' he said, 'my team, prompt for a change. Kaminsky, get me out of here.'

'Might not be as easy as last time, *boychik*,' Kaminsky said.

'Why not?'

Kaminsky sat across from Danny. I stood behind him.

'How'd you get Eddie in here?'

'He's Kaminsky's paid investigator.'

'Is that right?' Danny asked. 'Eddie, be careful, you might not think that's a promotion.'

'Danny,' I said, 'listen to Kaminsky.'

'What's it all about, Kaminsky?' Danny said. 'Why am I back here?'

'They got their ballistics report back on the bullet that killed Reynolds,' Kaminsky said.

Danny stiffened. 'And?'

'It matches your gun, Danny,' the lawyer said. 'You want to explain that one to me?'

Danny sat back in his chair. 'I can't.'

'Why not?'

'Because I don't know,' Danny said. 'I don't know how that's possible. I didn't kill him.'

'Danny—'

'Don't, Kaminsky,' Danny said. 'I know what you're gonna say. You can't help me if I don't tell you the truth.'

'That's right.'

'Well, I'm tellin' you the goddamned truth,' Danny said. 'I didn't kill Reynolds with my gun or any other gun. You've got to find out what the hell is going on.'

Kaminsky digested that and then said, 'I'll have to get myself a real investigator since you're my primary and you're in here.'

157

'You don't need anybody else,' Danny said. 'You've got Eddie.'

'Eddie?' Kaminsky asked. 'Come on, Danny, I just gave him a dollar to get him in here. I need a real detective.'

'Eddie's as good as anybody,' Danny said. 'He's a natural. Hell, he's learned from me.'

'Danny,' I said, 'listen to Kaminsky. I'm not a detective.'

'You've got everything it takes, Eddie,' he said, 'and you care about me. And with Jerry along, you guys make a great detective. I want you to clear me.'

I had butterflies in my stomach as I said, 'Jesus, buddy, you're puttin' your life in my hands.'

'Believe me when I say, there's nobody whose hands I'd rather have my life in than Eddie G.'s.' He looked at his lawyer. 'Kaminsky, make it happen.'

'You're killin' me, *boychik*,' Kaminsky said. He looked over his shoulder at me. 'You up to this?'

In front of Danny I couldn't say anything but: 'You bet I am.'

Danny would be arraigned the next morning, and it would be up to a judge to set bail – if he set bail. If not, then Danny would be behind bars until Kaminsky, Jerry and I could get him out.

On the street in front of the station Kaminsky

158

said, 'Get in your car and follow me.'

'Where are we going?'

'My office,' he said. 'we've got to talk strategy. You got the time?'

'Of course I've got the time.'

'I hope so,' he said. 'I hope you can give this all your attention, because it's gonna need it.'

'Don't worry, Kaminsky,' I said, 'I won't let Danny down.'

'Never mind Danny, *boychik*,' he said, 'don't even think about letting Kaminsky down.'

THIRTY-SIX

I got out of my car and looked at the building we stood in front of.

'This is your office?' I asked.

'My office is actually across the street,' he said, nodding his head toward an old four-story office building that had seen better days, 'but I spend most of my time here at Grabstein's Deli. And Kaminsky hasn't had breakfast yet. Have you?'

'No,' I said, realizing how hungry I was.

'OK,' he said, 'get ready for the best bagels and lox in Vegas.'

We went inside the deli and my mouth started to water because of all the wonderful smells. He was greeted like a long lost relative. Kaminsky led me to an orange booth, slid in and set his briefcase down next to him. I got in across from him.

'The usual, Manny,' he yelled, 'for Kaminsky and his friend.'

'Comin' up, Kaminsky.'

Manny was the cook – eighty if he was a day – and the plates were brought to the table by a woman almost as old. I assumed they were a couple.

There were bagels, lox, eggs (actually a pastrami omelet) and coffee.

'I have a friend who's going to be real mad when he hears about this,' I said.

'Someone Kaminsky will meet?'

'Definitely.'

'Well, then we'll bring him here another time,' Kaminsky said. 'Dig in.'

Growing up in Brooklyn I was familiar with bagels and lox. Although I lived in an Italian neighborhood, you only had to walk a block or two to get to a Jewish deli. I loved the hot dogs and knishes they sold, but I never developed a taste for lox, which is actually a piece of salmon filet. For breakfast? No thanks.

I took a heaped helping of the pastrami omelet and slathered a bagel with butter. While I was doing that the waitress came back with a bowl of home fries. Thank you, Lord. I took a couple of spoonfuls.

'No lox?' Kaminsky asked.

'No lox.'

'Suit yourself,' he said. 'More for Kaminsky.'

As we ate he said, 'I'm going to want to meet your whole team.'

'My team?'

'The people you'll be bringing in on this case,' Kaminsky said.

'Oh,' I said, 'well...'

161

'You do have somebody in mind, don't you?'

'Sure,' I said. 'In fact, you'd like him. His name is Jerry Epstein and he's from Brooklyn.'

'Excellent,' he said. 'A nice Jewish boy from, Brooklyn. The fella you said would be mad about you eating here?'

'Without him, yeah,' I said. 'He likes his food.'

'Kaminsky will see that he gets to eat here,' the lawyer said. 'Anybody else?'

'Maybe,' I said. 'I can use Penny—'

'Danny's Penny? Nice girl. Kaminsky likes her.'

'And I've got a few other people I can press into service,' I said.

He took a pad of paper from his briefcase, opened it and grabbed a pen.

'What are their names?'

'Well,' I said, 'Frank Sinatra, Dean Martin ... and Elvis Presley.'

'Frank Sin—' He stopped writing and looked up at me. 'What's the joke?'

'They're friends of mine,' I said, 'and they'll all help.'

'These are ... friends of yours?'

'Yep.'

He leaned forward.

'Are you talking about having your show business friends bring pressure to bear on the Las Vegas Police Department? Because Kaminsky doesn't need that kind of trouble. I could be disbarred.'

162

'No, no,' I said. 'They've just offered to help if I needed them.'

He sat back, picked up a piece of lox and popped it into his mouth.

'Anything else?' the waitress asked.

'A little glass of Manischewitz, Sima,' Kaminsky said.

'What? This early in the morning. Kaminsky, are you *Dafuk barosh?*'

'I need it,' Kaminsky said.

'All right. It's your funeral.'

She left the table to get his wine.

'What was that phrase she said?'

'Dafuk barosh?' he repeated. 'Oh, that's "fucked in the head".'

'Oh,' I said. 'And while we're at it ... what's schmaltz?'

THIRTY-SEVEN

Kaminsky drilled me on what he would need: a witness who saw someone else around the house at the time of the murder, whoever that other person was. Somebody else who wanted Reynolds dead. Somebody who wanted to frame Danny for murder. A gun.

'A gun?'

'If Danny's telling the truth and he didn't kill Reynolds, then somebody shot him.'

'With Danny's gun?'

'With a gun, certainly,' Kaminsky said.

'But the cops insist the bullet came from Danny's gun.'

'It's up to you to find out how that can be,' Kaminsky said. 'Or, more importantly, how it can't be. *Nu*?'

'Yeah,' I said, '*nu*.'

After breakfast we stopped briefly outside the deli.

'I'll hear from you soon?' he said.

'Very soon,' I said. 'And I'd like to know how the arraignment goes.'

'I have your number,' he said, patting his briefcase.

I had the feeling that the briefcase and deli were his *real* office, and that he kept the space in the building across the street as a mailing address.

'Eddie,' he said, 'Kaminsky is counting on you.'

'I know,' I said, 'I know. Kaminsky and Danny are counting on me. I get it.'

He put his hand on my shoulder.

'If this gets to be too much for you, call me,' he said. 'Understand?'

'I understand, Kaminsky.'

He patted my shoulder and then withdrew his hand.

'With such people as you have on your team,' he asked, waving his hand, 'how can we lose?'

'Right,' I said, 'how can we lose?'

I drove to the Sands. If I was going to save Danny's ass I had to put my 'team' together. I couldn't believe Danny was putting his life in my hands, but in truth, it had been in my hands before and he'd come out all right. So I had to stop doubting myself and get the job done.

When I got to the Sands I called Jerry first.

'Just checking to see if you were there,' I said. 'I'm comin' up.'

'Come ahead, Mr G.'

I took the elevator to Jerry's floor. He answered the door wearing one of his suits. Jerry always wore a suit, unless we were doing something at night or illegal ... or both.

'What's up, Mr G.?'

'Danny's been arrested again,' I said. 'This time they've got evidence.'

'What kinda evidence?'

'Ballistics,' I said. 'They claim the bullet that killed Reynolds came from Danny's gun.'

'What does Danny say?'

'He claims that's impossible.'

'So the lawyer, what's his name...?'

'Kaminsky.'

'Yeah, Kaminsky, he's got to prove that.'

'No,' I said, 'his investigator has to prove it.'

'And who's that?'

'You and me.'

'We gettin' paid?'

I took Kaminsky's dollar from my pocket and handed it to Jerry.

'There ya go.'

'OK,' he said, tucking the money in his pocket, 'as long as it's legal. Whatta we do first?'

'That's it?' I asked. 'That's your reaction?'

'Hey, Mr G.,' he said, with a shrug, 'if I was in a jam I'd call you. That's what Mr S. does, and Dino. Why would the Shamus be any different? Let's get to work.'

'Well, Kaminsky thinks I'm gonna put together a team.'

'You and me, that's the team,' he said.

'We need somebody in LA to track Billy Reynolds' movements, see if he crossed anybody who wants to kill him.'

'Who's gonna do that?'

'I'm gonna ask Frank to have it done,' I said. 'After all, he offered his help.'

'That's a good idea,' Jerry said. 'Mr S. has got connections.'

'Well,' I said, 'we're gonna put them to good use.'

THIRTY-EIGHT

When I called Frank he told me Dino was in his suite and we should come on up. Frank opened the door and Dino greeted us with a big smile.

'Eddie!' He gave me a hug, and Jerry a firm handshake. Of all the members of the Summit – the Rat Pack – I have always felt the most warmth from Dino. I can't explain it. Frank and I sort of bonded over the Frank Jr kidnapping thing, which I helped with, but there was still a warmth missing. But I could see that feeling on Frank's part for Dino. It was obvious that Frank needed Dino's friendship.

'We've got coffee,' Frank said. 'Believe it or not, it's even too early for Dino to start drinkin'.'

The jokes on stage and off were always about Dino's alcohol consumption when, in fact, he didn't drink that heavily, at all.

'Frank told me you're babysitting Elvis,' Dean said. 'Is he the nice kid Frank always says he is?'

'Yeah,' I said. 'He's decent and down home.

That wild hip-gyrating thing doesn't seem to transfer to his life.' I did think that Elvis was always 'on', especially with his crew of 'friends'. In my opinion, Elvis was only himself when he was alone. When he was with anyone else – even one person – he was 'Elvis!'

When we all had coffee cups we sat down with Frank and Dean on the sofa, Jerry and I on the armchairs.

'What's goin' on, Eddie?' Frank asked. 'Can we help?'

'Actually, the problem isn't Elvis,' I said. 'It's my buddy, Danny.'

'I thought that was taken care of,' Frank said.

'So did I, but this morning the cops arrested him again.' I told them about the new evidence.

'And your pal swears he didn't shoot the guy?' Dino asked.

'He does.'

'And you believe him?'

'I do.'

Dean shrugged and looked at Frank. 'Then that's good enough for us. What can we do?'

'I need to have the victim checked out in LA,' I said. 'I need to know what he was into, who he was associated with, and who might want him dead.'

'We can take care of that,' Frank said. 'We've got connections in LA.'

'What about here in town?' Dino asked.

'Jerry and I are going to split up. He'll see if

he can track down Reynolds' movements in Vegas.'

'And you?' Frank asked.

'I'm going the other way,' I said. 'Check out if Danny pissed off anyone who might have wanted to frame him for murder.'

'What about Elvis?' Frank asked. Of course he had to be concerned with that, because he'd offered me up to the Colonel as a favor.

'I'll talk with him,' I said. 'I have to tell you he's not as dumb or as simple as his country act makes him appear to be.'

'I never thought he was dumb,' Frank said, 'but simple...'

'Not that, either,' I said. 'He told me he knew that you and the Colonel cooked this up so I could babysit him.'

Frank looked surprised. 'OK, I see what you mean. Was he pissed?'

'Not at all,' I said. 'He used the leverage to get me to tell him about the murder.'

'So he's interested,' Dino said.

'Very.'

'Then maybe you can use that to keep him in line,' Dean said. 'You know, tell him you'll keep him informed.'

'I'll try that,' I said. 'In fact, I'll go from here to the Riv to talk to him. I'm sure I can get him to cooperate by stayin' out of trouble.'

'OK,' Frank said, 'Dean and I will get on the phone to LA and put some people on this guy. You wanna write down his particulars?'

I took out a Sands notepad and passed him the notes I'd made in Jerry's room.

'Already done.'

'Good.'

'Guys, I gotta thank you for pitchin' in, here,' I said. 'Danny's ass is really in a sling. I'm sure he's gonna appreciate it, too.'

'Forget it, Eddie,' Frank said.

'It's nice to be the ones helping for once,' Dean said, 'rather than the ones asking for help.'

We agreed that I would get in touch with them later in the day, and then Jerry and I left.

In the lobby Jerry asked, 'Who gets the Caddy?'

I answered by tossing him the keys.

THIRTY-NINE

I got a car from the Sands motor pool. All I had to do was clear it with Jack Entratter. As soon as he heard what was going on he gave his consent. He also asked me to keep him updated.

I drove to the Riviera, braved the crowds once again to get inside and announced myself at the front desk.

'Mr Presley is rehearsing in the Versailles showroom.'

'That's fine,' I said. 'I'll just go—'

'I'll need to announce you, sir.'

'Sure.'

He called ahead to the showroom and said someone would be out momentarily. Of course, it was Red.

'Hey Red!' I said. 'Great to see you.'

He didn't speak, just turned and started walking. I followed him through the lobby, down a hall that led to the showrooms. As we neared the Versailles I could hear music, and Elvis singing. When we got inside it started to feel surreal.

Here he was, Elvis the King, with a guitar around his neck, performing. It was almost like a private show for me because the room was empty except for those on stage with him and a few members of his Mafia in the seats.

He finished up a version of 'Viva Las Vegas' and stared out at his crew.

'How was that?'

'Great!'

'Cool, man!'

'Wonderful.'

I followed Red down the aisle and Elvis spotted us.

'Eddie, how did it sound to you?' he asked.

'I couldn't really hear it that well in the back, Elvis,' I said. 'I think you might need to adjust your volume.'

Elvis stared at his boys, who were scattered throughout the theater.

'Why didn't one of you guys notice that?' he demanded. 'Thanks, Eddie.' He turned to his band and said, 'Take five, boys.' He lifted his guitar from around his neck and set it down, then dropped down from the stage to give me a hug.

'What's up?' he asked. 'I thought we were gonna meet this afternoon?'

'Can we talk?' I asked. 'Alone?'

'Sure,' he said. 'Come on, we'll go sit in the back. If you couldn't hear me, nobody'll be able to hear us.'

We walked into the back while Red and the

boys moved to the front. This time instead of Red glaring at me, I got it from all of them. I did notice that Sonny wasn't there.

We sat in the back row with a seat between us. His brow was damp with sweat and he used a handkerchief that looked like silk to wipe it.

'What's up?' he asked.

'I have a problem,' I said, and told him about Danny being arrested and me being asked to investigate.

'That's great!' he said excitedly, when I finished.

'Well...'

'No,' he said, 'I don't mean it's great that your friend got arrested again, I just mean it's great that you're the guy who's gonna help him.'

'OK,' I said, 'but this means I won't be able to spend as much time with you as I wanted to.'

'You mean as much time as the Colonel wanted you to.'

'Well, yeah.'

'You said Frank and Dean are helpin'?'

'That's right,' I said. 'They offered and I needed to accept.

'OK, then,' he said, 'that's the answer.'

'What's the answer?'

'I'm gonna be part of your team,' he said. 'I'm goin' out with you.'

When I gave Kaminsky Elvis' name as part of my team I admit I was showing off. I never expected that Elvis would actually want to help.

'Now wait a minute,' I said. 'I'm supposed to keep you out of trouble, not take you into a murder investigation.'

'What's a better way to keep an eye on me than to take me with you?' he asked.

'You have that thing this afternoon, remember,' I said.

'We can go together, and after that we can get to work,' he proposed.

'Elvis, the Colonel would kill me—'

'He'll kill you if I tell him you blew me off.'

'You wouldn't.'

'Well,' he said, 'I wouldn't want to ... come on, Eddie. I want in. I've never done anything like this before.'

'You're gonna be recognized...'

'I'll wear a hat and sunglasses,' he said. 'I swear, nobody'll know it's me.'

I wondered how he was gonna cover up those sideburns.

FORTY

I spoke to Kaminsky just before lunch that morning. The arraignment hadn't gone well. The judge had set bail for Danny at two million dollars.

'What?'

'And he considered it charitable for a charge of murder,' Kaminsky said. 'Don't worry, Kaminsky's looking for a bondsman that will put up the ten per cent.'

'OK,' I said. 'Let me know how it goes.'

The afternoon thing was a meet and greet with the press. They had it in the Versailles. I stood in the back of the room while the reporters fired questions at Elvis, Ann-Margret and another actor, Cesare Danova. Poor Danova, he was virtually ignored while Elvis and Ann-Margret answered most of the questions. Despite the fact that he was an actor with many roles under his belt, he took it all in good humor, recognizing the fact that Elvis was the star.

When it was over a limo took Ann-Margret

and Cesare Danova to their hotels. Elvis came to the back of the theater and sat next to me.

'I'm all yours,' he said. 'What do we do first?'

I looked at him and said, 'We get you a hat.'

In the lobby of the hotel, I bought Elvis a baseball cap with LAS VEGAS written on it. If I had the chance I'd replace it with something more innocuous. He put on a pair of sunglasses and, to me, he looked like Elvis Presley with glasses and a hat. Maybe it would work on others, though.

We went out the back door to the rear parking lot of the Riviera, where I had left the car.

'This is yours?' he asked, looking at the 1960 Ford Falcon.

'No, I got it from the Sands,' I said. 'I'm lettin' Jerry use my Caddy.'

'Jerry,' Elvis said. 'Where is he? Isn't he workin' with us?'

'He's workin' on the other aspect of the case,' I said, as we got in the car. 'He's checking on what Reynolds was doing in town. We're gonna check up on what Danny's been workin' on.' I'd given Jerry a location to meet us at in about three hours, hoping that was enough time for all of us to find out something.

'You think he's workin' on a case where somebody wants to kill him?'

'Frame him, is more likely.'

'But to frame him, wouldn't somebody need

177

to know about this guy Reynolds?'

'You're right,' I said. 'That's a good point, Elvis.'

I pulled the car out of the parking lot.

'Where we headed?' he asked.

'Fremont Street,' I said. 'I'm gonna take another look at Danny's office.'

When we got to Fremont Street the downstairs door was open. I remembered locking it, so either Danny or Penny had left it open. Or Penny was upstairs.

We went up, found that door unlocked, too. When we entered, Penny was sitting at her desk.

'What are you doin' here?' I asked.

'I couldn't just sit home. Did Kaminsky tell you about the arraignment?'

'Yes, he did.'

'I was making some calls, trying to find someone who would put up the bail.'

'Any luck?'

'No,' she said. 'I guess you find out who your friends are when you're asking them for money.'

'How much money?' Elvis asked.

Penny looked up and I could see that she didn't recognize him.

'Who's he?' she asked me.

'Him? That's ... Buzz.'

'Buzz?'

'Yeah, he's helpin' out.'

178

'Where's Jerry?'

'He's doin' somethin' else.'

'How much money is needed, ma'am?' Elvis asked.

'Well ... Buzz ... the bail is two million dollars,' she said. 'A bondsman only needs to put up two hundred thousand dollars. Do you think you have two hundred thousand dollars?'

'As a matter of fact, I do,' Elvis said.

She stared at him.

'You mean it?' I asked him.

'Well, sure,' he said. 'What good's money if you can't use it to help your friends?'

'Is he serious?' Penny asked.

'I think he is,' I said.

'But—'

'Take off your hat ... Buzz,' I said.

FORTY-ONE

'Buzz?' Penny asked, moments later.

'Best I could come up with on short notice.' Elvis looked at her sheepishly.

'Elvis Presley?' she said, for the third time.

'Are you serious about putting up the bail money for Danny?' I asked, again.

'Well, sure,' he said. 'I told you I'd help, didn't I?'

'Oh, Mr Presley...' Penny said.

'Ma'am, I'd appreciate it if you'd just call me Elvis.'

'All right, Elvis.'

'Penny, call Kaminsky,' I said. 'He'll have a bondsman we can use. Tell him we've got the money. But don't tell him where from.'

'OK, Eddie.'

'Why not tell 'im?' Elvis asked.

'We don't want it getting out that you're involved,' I said. 'If that happened the Colonel would really have my head.'

'You're probably right.'

'We'll have to go to a bank to get cash,' I said, 'but we don't want a check floating

180

around with your name on it.'

'We can do that later,' Elvis said. 'What about the reason we came?'

'When Penny gets off the phone I'll have her show me Danny's active files.'

'Why just active?' Elvis asked.

'We have to start somewhere.'

'Eddie?' Penny held the phone out to me. 'Kaminsky wants to talk to you.'

I grabbed the phone.

'Eddie, here.'

'Where did you find two hundred grand?' Kaminsky asked.

'I work in a casino, remember?' I said. 'I know people with money.'

'One of your show business friends?'

'I'm not gonna say, Kaminsky,' I said. 'Just know that I've got it.'

'OK,' he said, 'just bring it to my office later today.'

'Your office, or—'

'Grabstein's,' he said, and hung up.

'Is it OK?' Penny asked.

'It will be,' I assured her. 'I'll bring him the money later, but first we need to take a look at Danny's active cases.'

'That's easy,' she replied. 'He was only working on one.'

She walked to her file cabinet, looked inside, then closed it. 'He must have it on his desk.'

She thought Danny was working on one case.

181

What she didn't know was that she was the second one. I still hadn't gotten a good explanation from Danny as to why he had asked me to help with following Penny, but that was going to have to come later.

Penny went into Danny's office with Elvis and me following. She walked around behind the desk, and came up with a file.

'This is it,' she said, handing it to me.

'I'll read this,' I said. 'But first break it down for me, Penny.'

Albert Kroner was missing.

Kroner was a lawyer with a practice in Chicago. He had apparently absconded with the fortunes of several of his high profile clients. Danny was hired to try and locate him in Las Vegas.

'Why Las Vegas?' I asked Penny.

'It's just one place his clients think he may have run to. They got together and hired several private investigators here, and in a few European countries he might have gone.'

'What has Danny found out?'

'I don't know,' Penny said. 'Whatever he's found will be in that file. He hasn't discussed it with me, but then I haven't exactly been ... accessible.'

'I understand.'

'So you think this fella Kroner framed him for murder?' Elvis asked.

'How could he?' Penny asked. 'How would

182

he know anything about Billy Reynolds and me?'

'I don't know,' I said. 'I'll ask him when we find him.'

'How are you going to do that?' she asked.

'By getting some help from Chicago.'

FORTY-TWO

Jerry pulled the Caddy to a stop in front of the house and got out. It was a two-story A-frame in a middle class residential neighborhood far off the strip. From what Jerry and I had heard, Reynolds had rented the house, but we didn't know who from.

Jerry approached the front door, which had been sealed with police tape. He knew he could break the tape, but he was sure I didn't want the cops to know we'd been there. He decided to find another way in.

He walked around to the side of the house, along a hedge that stood about six feet tall. When he looked over the hedge he stopped short at what he saw. A woman was sun bathing in her back yard, lying on a chaise lounge face down, nude. The hedge was supposed to offer her privacy, but Jerry was tall enough to see over it.

Her skin was white, as if she'd just started the tanning process. In Jerry's opinion, she had a great ass, plump as a fresh pear, and although she was lying on them, he could tell she had a top drawer pair of tits.

'Mr G.,' he told me later, 'it was like I was nailed to the floor.'

I told him I couldn't blame him if she was the babe he said she was.

She turned her head and saw him, staring at her over the hedge.

'What are you standing on?' she asked.

'Wha ... uh, nothing. Just my feet.'

'You're that tall?'

'I guess so.'

She pushed herself up on one elbow, so he could see one large breast with a cherry nipple.

'It wasn't really a cherry, Mr G.,' he said, 'it just reminded me of one.'

I told him I got it.

'You a cop?' she asked, looking amused. Jerry said she was no kid, maybe thirty-six or so, but still a dish.

'No, ma'am.'

'"No ma'am"?' she repeated. 'But you are interested in the murder that took place in that house, right?'

'Yes, ma ... uh, yes.'

'Why?'

'I'm, uh, an investigator for a lawyer.'

'You don't look like an investigator,' she said.

'What do I look like?'

She studied him for a moment, cocking her head to one side, then said, 'Muscle.'

'That, too.'

'What's your name?'

'Jerry.'

'Hi, Jerry, I'm Amanda. Come on around and we'll talk.'

'You know somethin' about the murder?' he asked.

'I know something,' she said. 'Come on.' She sat up straighter, so he could clearly see her pendulous breasts. He said they swayed when she moved. 'I won't bite.'

Jerry said by the time he found his way around the hedge to her back yard she had put on a two-piece bathing suit that hardly covered her.

'You didn't think I was gonna stay naked and talk to you, did ya?' she asked.

'I was hopin',' he answered, honestly.

She laughed. 'You're cute. Come inside where it's cool. I'll give you a drink.'

She led the way into her house, which was a split level rather than a real two floor. They stepped down as she led him into a dining room.

'What'll you have?' she asked. 'Lemonade or ice tea?'

'No booze?' he asked.

'I don't drink,' she said. She turned and looked at him. 'Just because I sun bathe in the raw don't make me a bad girl, mister.'

'Sorry,' he said. 'I didn't mean nothin'. I'll take lemonade.'

'Sit at the table. I'll bring it.'

She went into the kitchen. When she reappeared she was holding two icy glasses of lemonade, and wearing an almost see-through thing that covered her to the waist. Sort of.

'Here,' she said. She handed him a glass, sat across the table from him. 'I knew Billy Reynolds. He'd been renting that house for about two months.'

'Knew him how well?'

'Not that well, cowboy,' she said.

'I didn't mean that,' he said. 'I just meant—'

'OK, never mind. I'll stop takin' offense if you stop apologizing.'

'Deal.'

'I'm gonna tell you what I know,' she said, 'things I didn't tell the cops. You wanna know why?'

'Sure.'

'You've got a nice face,' she said. 'That detective, Hargrove, he's kind of a prick.'

'I know him,' Jerry said, 'and you're right. He is a prick.'

'Good,' she said. 'I'm still a good judge of men, then. I'm here divorcing one.'

'So you don't own this house?'

'No,' she said, 'I'm renting it, just like Billy was.'

'From the same person?' he asked.

'From the same realtor.'

'Got a name?'

'Don't worry, I'll give you a name and address before you leave.'

'Thanks.' He sipped the lemonade. It was

fresh made.

'I've been here about six weeks,' she said. 'Bill was already here. We had a few drinks and he told me he was working on a big deal. I figured he was talking big, trying to get into my pants. He didn't, by the way.'

'I didn't think so.'

She smiled.

'You see anybody come to the house?'

'It was a girl. Pretty young thing, dark hair in a ponytail. She went in, came out a few minutes later cryin'.'

'Anybody else?'

'A man,' she said. 'Tall – not as tall as you – handsome, in his forties.'

'Did he go in?'

'He did, came out a few minutes later,' she said, 'like the girl. Only he wasn't cryin'. He was just boilin' mad.'

'Did this happen on the same day?'

'Yup,' she said. 'The day of the murder.'

'What about the past six weeks,' Jerry asked, 'before that day. See anybody?'

'Well,' she said, 'it's not like I just sit around here all day. I do go to the casinos.'

'I figured.'

'He really didn't have that many visitors until just the other day,' she said.

'The man who came and left mad?' Jerry asked, 'did you see his car? Get his license plate number?'

'Not me,' she said. 'That would be the nosy

188

neighbor across the street. She's the one who gave that information to the cops.'

'Which house?'

'The horrible yellow, straight across from Billy's. She's the nosiest bitch. I can't walk out of the house without her curtain suddenly bein' pushed aside.'

'She got a name?'

'Nosy, as far as I know,' she said. 'I don't get to know the neighbors – well, except Billy, a little, but we were both renting.'

Jerry finished his lemonade, then put the glass down and stood up.

'Leavin' so soon?' she asked.

'I got work to do,' he said. 'I'll have to talk to the nosy neighbor. Don't worry. I won't mention you.'

'I don't care if you do,' she said. 'I'll walk you out.'

She wrote the name of the realtor on a slip of paper for Jerry, then walked him to the front door. She opened it and stepped out onto the porch with him. She folded her arms over her generous breasts.

'Thanks for talkin' to me, Jerry. I do get lonely.'

Either Jerry missed a chance, or she was telling the truth and wasn't coming on to him, at all. Maybe the woman really did just want somebody to talk to.

'Thanks, Amanda,' he said. 'For the information.'

'Billy wasn't a bad guy,' she said, 'at least, to me. I don't know what his big deal was, but even if it was crooked, I don't think he deserved to die.'

'Maybe not,' Jerry said. 'Yellow house, right?'

'Right,' Amanda said, 'and don't worry, she knows you're comin'. She's watchin' us right now.'

FORTY-THREE

Jerry went across the street to the one-story yellow A-frame that looked like one of the oldest houses on the block. He stepped to the door and rang the bell; the curtain in the window rustled.

There was a small window in the door and he saw a woman's wrinkled face appear in it.

'Whataya want?'

'Just to talk, ma'am,' Jerry said. 'I'm investigatin' the murder that happened across the street.'

The woman unlocked the door in haste and opened it. She was short, dressed in a housecoat, looked about sixty-five, with mousy grey hair and a mug full of wrinkles.

'Don't believe nothin' she tells you!' she snapped.

'Who?'

'That hoochie-coochie girl over there,' she said. 'She didn't see nothin' I did.'

'What did you see, ma'am?'

'I saw the killer and his car.'

'What'd he look like?'

'Dark hair, kinda handsome. Tall, but not as tall as you.'

'What kind of car.'

'Don't know kinds,' she said. 'It was dark. But I gave the police the license number.'

'Do you still have it?' he asked.

'Sure do, right here.' She reached over and grabbed a pad of paper from a small table.

'Can I keep this?' he asked.

'The other cops already got it,' she said. 'That nice detective actually helped me decide if one of the letters was a G or a C.'

'He did, huh?'

'And one of the numbers was either a four, or maybe an A.'

Jerry tore a blank page from her pad, handed it back, and scribbled some notes.

'Thanks, ma'am.'

'Hey, detective,' she said, as he went back down the stairs, 'you never showed me your badge.'

'Ain't got one.'

'All cops got badges.'

He turned his head and tossed his last comment over his shoulder.

'I never said I was a cop!'

Jerry had almost reached the Caddy when he heard his name. He turned and saw Amanda running toward him. She was trying to hold that filmy wrap together, but still managed to jiggle quite a bit as she ran up to him.

'I just remembered something,' she said,

slightly out of breath.

'What?'

'A few weeks ago I was out in the yard when I heard some shouting from Billy's house. I walked over to the hedge, a spot where I can see through.'

'And?'

'He was arguing with a man in his living room.'

'How good a look did you get at the man?'

'Not real good,' she said.

'Was it the same man?'

'I didn't see him real well, but I don't think so. I mean, he had dark hair, and when I looked out front there was a dark car. But I don't think it was the same.'

'Did you see the license plate of the car?'

'No, I'm sorry,' she said. 'I just don't notice things like that.'

'OK, Amanda,' he said. 'Thank you.'

'You're a nice man, Jerry,' she said to him. 'Come back and see me some time.'

'Sure,' he said, 'sure I will.'

FORTY-FOUR

While Jerry was dallying with the ladies, Elvis and I went to the bank.

We had to go into a private room where Elvis could remove his hat and glasses, and also produce his ID. Then he had to make a call to the Colonel and tell him what he'd agreed to do. As I expected, the Colonel asked to speak to me.

'Mr Gianelli, this isn't what I expected when I asked you to look out for Elvis.'

'It's not what I expected either, Colonel, but circumstances have placed us here.'

'Does Elvis know this friend of yours?' he asked.

'No,' I admitted, 'I suspect that he's doing this as a favor to me.'

'This is an expensive favor.'

'No argument from me.'

He'd probably think it was even more expensive if he knew that Elvis was out investigating with me. We'd kept that part from him.

'Very well,' he said, 'put the boy back on.'

The upshot was we walked out of the bank with a check certified for two hundred thousand dollars.

'Pastrami?' Kaminsky asked. 'Best in town.'

'No,' I said, thinking of Jerry again. Now I'd been to a Jewish deli twice without him.

'No,' Elvis said, 'thank you, kindly.'

If Kaminsky was impressed by Elvis' presence he didn't show it. Maybe rock 'n roll wasn't his kind of music. But he was impressed when we handed the check over to him.

'I'll get this into my account today,' he said. 'I have a bondsman waiting.'

We could have made the check out to the bondsman, but Kaminsky didn't have his name ready when we talked.

Elvis and I did both agree to a can of Dr Brown's soda, cream for me, orange for him. We both sipped.

'So, how's the investigation going?' Kaminsky asked, biting into his pastrami-on-rye. Mustard popped out the back and landed on the table.

'OK,' I said, 'we've got some info on Danny's live case, and Jerry's collecting some facts about Billy Reynolds and why he may have been in town. We're also checking on Reynolds' movements in LA to see who he might-'ve pissed off.'

'Good, good,' Kaminsky said. 'Just keep workin' and keep me informed. Kaminsky is workin' on a defense strategy.'

'I thought the strategy was that Danny didn't do it?' I commented.

'The ballistics match is going to be hard to circumvent,' Kaminsky said. 'If we could de-bunk that match we'd have a viable defense.'

'Well then,' I said, 'that's where we'll put the bulk of our efforts.'

'Fine, fine.'

We stood up to leave.

'It was a pleasure meeting you, Mr Presley,' Kaminsky said.

Elvis put his sunglasses back on – he'd left the hat on his head – and said, 'The name's Buzz.'

Outside, as we got into the car, Elvis asked me, 'Where did you come up with Buzz?'

'It just came to me on the spur of the moment,' I said. 'We can change it if you like.'

'Na, na, na,' Elvis said, 'I like it. Stroke of genius. I'm gonna use it while we're tourin'. You know, when I wanna go out without anybody knowin' who I really am.'

We got in and slammed the doors.

'Where to?' he asked.

'We've gotta meet Jerry and hope he's turned up something.'

As we drove he asked, 'What did the Colonel say?'

'Just something about you doing me an ex-pensive favor,' I said. 'I'm afraid he might be thinking that I'm taking advantage of you.'

'I been taken advantage of before,' Elvis said. 'I know what it feels like and trust me, this ain't it.'

'Thanks, Elvis.'

'Hey, we're partners, right?'

'Right.'

And as a result of the huge favor, we were going to stay that way till the end.

Who was taking advantage of who here?

FORTY-FIVE

Jerry, Elvis and I sat in a small diner near my house that I sometimes ate breakfast in. I wanted to keep 'Buzz' away from the strip.

When Jerry walked in he didn't blink at Elvis' appearance.

'We eatin'?' he asked.

'Order whatever you want.'

Elvis wanted a banana-and-peanut butter sandwich, which I talked him out of. It was too unusual and would attract attention. I suggested burger platters for all of us, and that's what we went with.

'OK, Jerry what did you get?' I asked.

That was when he told us his story about Amanda and the nosy lady.

'Let me see the license plate number,' I said.

He took out the notes he'd made and passed them over. The waitress appeared with our plates and we leaned back to allow her to set them down. She took a second look at us but didn't say anything. When she was gone I put the paper on the table to examine. Elvis leaned over as he plucked a French fry from his plate.

'Look at this,' I said. 'With the 4 and the G, it's Danny's plate number. But put in the A or the C and it belongs to somebody else.'

'But who?' Elvis asked.

'We're going to find out,' I said, folding the paper and tucking it into my pocket. 'It sounds to me like Hargrove steered this lady toward Danny's plate number.'

'Yeah, that's what I thought,' Jerry said, around a huge bite of hamburger.

'We'll find somebody to run these other plates and see who they match.'

'If we find out it was somebody else's car, won't that clear him?' Elvis asked.

'Afraid not,' I said. 'There's still the gun.'

'What about the gun?' Elvis asked.

'The cops say the bullet that killed Reynolds came from Danny's gun.'

'And he says it didn't?'

'That's right.'

'And you believe him?'

'Completely.'

'Then we need to find the gun that did kill him.'

'Exactly,' I said.

'Or who used Danny's gun,' Jerry said.

We both looked at him. Jerry always manages to fool people – even me – about how smart he was.

'Danny doesn't always carry his gun,' I said. 'I've got to find out if he had it on him that day.'

'Does he have another one?' Jerry asked. 'I mean, I got more than one gun, even though I use a forty-five most of the time.'

'Yeah, he does,' I said. 'I don't know how many, or what kind. But Penny probably does.'

'Maybe not,' Jerry said. 'A man usually keeps his guns to himself.'

'That's true,' Elvis agreed.

'You got guns?' Jerry asked.

'I got lots of guns,' Elvis said. He took off his sunglasses. 'You come to Graceland sometime and I'll show you around.'

'That would be great.'

The waitress came over, edging closer rather than just walking up, and peering at Elvis.

'I, uh, hey,' she said, 'are you ... are you him? Are you ... Elvis Presley?'

He put his glasses back on and said, 'You know, I get that a lot.' He smiled at her. 'My name's Buzz.'

As we left the diner Jerry said, 'Buzz?'

'Just came up with it,' I said.

'I like it,' Elvis said. 'It's nice and simple. And you know what? So's Buzz. His whole life is simple.'

'You'd rather be Buzz?' Jerry asked.

'Sometimes,' Elvis said. 'Yeah, sometimes I would.'

Elvis got in the car, closed the door.

'Whataya want me to do now, Mr G.?' Jerry asked.

'Is it OK if you go and talk to the realtor?' I asked.

'Well, yeah,' he said, 'why you gotta ask me that?'

'I don't want you to think I'm sendin' you on errands.'

'Hey, we're partners, right?' he said. 'I'll talk to the realtor.'

'You did good with those women,' I said.

'The realtor's a guy,' he said. 'I do better with guys. They're afraid of me.'

'Women aren't?'

'Not unless I make 'em,' he said. 'Women know I ain't gonna hit 'em or nothin' – not unless I have to.'

I wasn't sure I wanted to hear about that part of his business.

'Well,' I said, 'don't hit anybody unless you absolutely have to.'

'OK, Mr G.'

He walked to the Caddy and got in. I went around and got behind the wheel of my borrowed car.

'I made a mistake in there,' Elvis said.

'What mistake?'

'Took off my shades, let my guard down,' he explained. 'That waitress recognized me.'

'You convinced her you were Buzz,' I said. 'No harm done.'

'You got a friend dependin' on you,' Elvis said. 'I shouldn't be messin' with that, except...'

'Except what?'

He turned his head, looked at me from behind those glasses and beneath that hat.

'Well, today I kinda felt like his life depended on me, too,' he said. 'I ain't never felt nothin' like that before. What I do ain't so danged important. I kinda liked it.'

'Well,' I said, 'keep on liking it. I kinda like havin' you around, so I'm not about to cut you loose now.'

He studied me for a minute, then nodded and said, 'Well, all right.'

FORTY-SIX

'I have to read this file,' I said, as we drove.

'Let's go to your house,' Elvis said. 'I wanna see it.'

'It's no Graceland, my friend.'

'Remember, I told you about my house in Tupelo,' he said. 'I'm sure yours is very nice.'

I shrugged, turned the car toward my street.

We pulled up in front and Elvis took a good look.

'I would have been very happy to live in a house like this,' he said. 'I bought Graceland so I could take my mama and father in with me. She died before she could really enjoy it.'

'What did she think of it?' I asked, as we got out of the car.

'She was overwhelmed,' Elvis said. 'I think she probably would have preferred a house like this one.'

I unlocked the front door and we went in. Frank, Dino and Sammy had all been to my house at one time. Now Elvis Presley.

'Yes,' he said, looking around my small but – thankfully – clean living room, 'she would have loved this. Is that the kitchen?'

'Yes.'

He went in, looked around, then came back.

'You've done OK for yourself, Eddie,' he said. 'It's comfortable. It's ... a home.'

'It's good for me,' I said. 'I'll make some coffee and then read the file.'

'Let's both read it,' Elvis said. 'I want to know what you know.'

'Fine,' I said. 'Here, you start while I make the coffee.'

He took the file, sat down on the sofa and opened it.

I came back to the living room with two cups of coffee to find Elvis leaning over the coffee table, the contents of the file spread out before him.

'Thanks,' he said, accepting the coffee. He had set aside the hat and dark glasses.

I sat down next to him, a cushion between us, and looked at the contents of the file. There were even some photos.

'Whataya got?' I asked.

'You're gonna read it,' he said.

'I know, but give me your thoughts.'

'Well,' Elvis said, 'your friend Danny has photos of three men he thinks might be this fella Albert Kroner.'

'He can't tell?'

'According to his notes,' Elvis said, 'he thinks Kroner may have had some plastic surgery. These three men physically match his description.'

'Are they all here, in Las Vegas?'

Elvis leaned over to look at something.

'One here, one in Lake Tahoe, and one some-place called Laughlin?'

'South of here,' I said. 'Small gambling town on the river.'

'Looks like he had an original list of eight possibles,' Elvis said, 'and he's whittled it down to these three.'

He sat back, sipped his coffee.

'I need a shower,' he said. 'Those press things always make me sweat.'

'Help yourself,' I said. 'I don't think I have any pants that'll fit you, but I bet you can find a shirt.'

'Thanks. I'll take this with me.'

'I'll give the file a read myself while you're doing that.'

'Be right back.'

I pointed and said, 'Right through there.'

He went into my bedroom and I started reading. I got pretty much the same thing out of it that Elvis had. Danny had three suspects he thought could be Albert Kroner. He had been planning to do a thorough investigation into each. What I didn't know was whether or not he was going to go to Laughlin and Tahoe him-self, or farm those jobs out.

I sat back, lifted the cup to my lips and realiz-ed it was empty. I went back to the kitchen for more.

The phone rang before I got out of the kitchen. I picked up the wall unit and said, 'This is Eddie.'

'Eddie, it's Frank.'

'Hey, Frank. What's up?'

'Dino and I have some info for you,' he said. 'You better come on over and get it, though.'

'The Sands?'

'Right.'

'OK,' I said, 'we'll be there soon.'

'We? Jerry with you?'

'No,' I said. 'Elvis.'

'Hey, crazy,' Frank said. 'Yeah, bring 'im over. I'll order up.'

'OK,' I said, 'give us half an hour.'

'Bye, Clyde.'

As I hung up, Elvis came walking in.

'This one OK?' he asked, modeling the T-shirt he'd grabbed. It was green and said UNLV on it. Someone had given it to me in '62, when the University of Las Vegas was first formed.

'That's fine,' I said. 'More coffee?'

'We got time? You were tellin' somebody we'd be there in half an hour.'

'Yeah, we got time,' I said. 'I'm gonna wash up and then we've got to go to the Sands. Frank and Dino have something for us.'

'Hey, I'd like to see those guys,' Elvis said.

'And they'd like to see you,' I said. 'Gimme a minute and then we'll go. Have some more coffee.'

He was pouring himself a cup as I left, carrying mine into the bedroom. I washed up in the sink and changed out of the suit I was wearing into a T-shirt and jeans.

'Ready to go?' I asked.

Elvis had collected the file off the table and put it back together.

'I'm ready.'

FORTY-SEVEN

Frank opened the door and he and Elvis grinned and gave each other a hug.

'How you doin', kid?'

'Just fine, sir.'

'Drop that sir stuff,' Frank said. 'It's Frank, remember?'

'Sure, Frank.'

'Hey, Eddie,' Frank said.

'Frank.'

He closed the door and waved. 'We ordered up some food. Dino's tendin' bar.'

We walked into the suite and Dino waved from behind the bar.

'What'll ya have, boys?' he asked. 'Let's have a drink before we eat.'

There was a cart on wheels in a corner with some covered dishes.

Elvis approached the bar and stuck his hand out.

'Nice to meet you, sir.'

'Dean,' Dino said, 'just call me Dean. Nice to meet you too, kid. Hey, Eddie. Drinkin'?'

'Bourbon,' I said.

'Elvis?'

'Pepsi, if you've got it.'

'We got it.'

Frank, Elvis and I sat at the bar while Dino laid out some drinks, his ever present cigarette in his right hand. He may not have drunk to his reputation, but he smoked like a chimney.

Frank, Dino and Elvis talked music for a few minutes before we got down to business. I told Frank and Dino what we'd found out, what Jerry had told us, and about Elvis putting up Danny's bail.

'That was damn nice of you, Elvis,' Frank said.

'We can pitch it so you don't have to foot the whole bill,' Dino said. 'In fact, Eddie, you should've asked us.'

'For what? Two hundred thousand dollars? I'd never do that, Dean.' I would have accepted it, but I never would have asked for it.

'The Sands might have put it up,' Frank said.

'I wouldn't ask Jack for that, either,' I said. 'This worked out fine. As long as Danny does not skip town, Elvis will get his money back. So, what was it you guys wanted to tell me?'

Frank and Dean exchanged a glance.

'What is it?' I asked.

'You guys want me to leave?' Elvis asked.

'No, no,' Frank said, 'you can hear this, too.'

'Eddie,' Dino said, 'we made a few calls, and found out that your man Reynolds was hanging

209

around in LA with Joey Scaffazza.'

'Why don't I like the sound of this?' I asked.

'Scaffazza,' Frank said, 'worked for Johnny Roselli.'

'Oh, great,' I said. Roselli was the boss of the LA Mafia. But he was also a friend of Frank's. Frank had sponsored Roselli to become a member of the Friar's Club.

'Frank—'

'I know what you're gonna say,' Frank said. 'I'm flyin' to LA tomorrow to see Johnny and see what I can find out.'

'Thanks.'

'I've got to warn you, though,' Frank said. 'These guys are your friends as long as it does not hurt them. We can't depend on Johnny talkin' to me just because we're friends.'

'I get it.'

'This sounds like dangerous stuff,' Elvis said.

'Murder's always dangerous, kid,' Frank said.

'Yes, sir.'

I marveled at the way Elvis always maintained respect for whoever he was speaking with. But I had spent hours with him now and I had seen the intelligence behind his eyes. He rarely spoke impulsively, thought about his answers to questions, whether he was on stage, or speaking in private.

'You going to LA, Dino?' I asked.

Dean shook his head.

'Frank's going to talk to Johnny alone. Why, you need something else?'

'Well,' I said, 'I do need somebody to go to Lake Tahoe...'

FORTY-EIGHT

The next morning Elvis and I were on the road, driving to Laughlin. Frank had taken his jet to LA, while Dino had taken the Sands helicopter to Lake Tahoe. Jerry was going to check on Danny's suspect in Vegas.

One of my 'team' had to find out which man was Albert Kroner. But Frank's task was a little different. He was going to try to find out what – if anything – Johnny Roselli had to say about William Reynolds. Of all our tasks, I was most interested in his...

Frank landed at LAX. He had already called Roselli to make an appointment, and the gangster had agreed to see him. They decided to meet at Musso's & Frank's Grill, on Hollywood Blvd.

Musso's was Old Hollywood. All of the greats had eaten there, not only Hollywood's elite actors like the Barrymores and Charlie Chaplin, but writers like Raymond Chandler, Jim Thompson and Budd Schulberg, who used to take breaks from writing his book *What*

Makes Sammy Run to eat at Musso's.

And, of course, Frank, Sammy, Dino and Joey were seen there all the time. Johnny Roselli, who thought he was a Hollywood star, looked and dressed the part, and showed up in all the right places. He was already seated in a red leather booth when Frank arrived.

'Hello, Johnny,' Frank said, shaking the gangster's hand.

'Frank,' Roselli said. 'How you doin'?'

'Great,' Frank said, sitting across from Roselli in the U-shaped booth. 'You're lookin' good.'

Roselli patted his stomach and said, 'I like to stay fit.' His silver hair was slicked back and he had a deep tan which he thought made him look younger. He was impeccably turned out in a five-hundred-dollar suit.

'I was sorry to hear about what happened to Frank Jr last year,' Roselli said. 'I called, but I couldn't come around...'

'I know,' Frank said, 'the cops and FBI were all over me. I understand, Johnny, and I appreciate the thought.'

This was the Frank and Johnny dance that went on all the time. I truly believe they thought of each other as friends, showing the proper respect. But they really just had a use for each other. In fits of rage I'd heard Frank refer to Roselli as 'that puffed up blowhard', and years later discovered that Roselli had often referred to Frank as 'that fuckin'

213

lounge singer.'

But on this day they were two friends meeting for lunch.

After Aurelio, the waiter, took their orders and brought Martinis, Johnny Roselli said, 'What's this about, Frank? I mean, it's always nice to see you, but you said you had a problem.'

'Actually,' Frank said, 'a friend of mine in Vegas has the problem and, you know me, I'm always tryin' to help.'

'That's true, Frank.' Roselli said. 'I'm the same way.'

'I know that, Johnny,' Frank said. 'That's why I called you.'

They leaned back and allowed the waiter to set down their lunches. Frank had the fried calamari, Roselli a plate of mussels and clams.

'So here's the problem,' Frank said.

'Frank,' Roselli said, 'can we put this off until we eat? I mean, come on, *paisan*, look at this food, eh? It deserves our full attention, no?'

'You're right, Johnny,' Frank said. 'When you're right, you're right.' Frank told me later that the best way to handle Roselli was to keep telling him he was right.

So they ate, and only exchanged small talk for the next twenty minutes.

Roselli sat back twenty-three minutes later and patted his stomach.

'Thanks to you I'm gonna have to work this off, Frankie,' he said.

'Worth it, though, huh, Johnny?' Frank asked.

'Look at you, ya mook,' Roselli said. 'You're like a rail no matter what you eat. *Fongool*!'

Frank had no answer for that.

'Let's have some dessert. We can talk over that.'

They had coffee and pastries, *sfogliatelle* and *cannolis*.

'OK, *paisan*,' Roselli said, 'what's it about, this trouble a friend of yours has in Vegas?'

'It has to do with a guy named William Reynolds,' Frank said. 'You know him?'

'Reynolds,' Roselli said, frowning. 'That don't ring a bell, Frank.'

'Supposedly he hung around with Joey Scaffazza.'

'Scaffazza?' Roselli said. 'That scumbag? That *pompinara.*' Frank knew Roselli had to dislike the guy to call him a cocksucker. Or wanted Frank to think he disliked him.

'Then you know him.'

'Yeah, he used to work for me,' Roselli said. 'I fired his worthless ass when I found out he was in business for himself. If it was the old days I woulda ... ah, never mind. If your friend was mixed up with Scaffazza there's no tellin' what they was into.'

'Look, Johnny, I want to level with you,' Frank said. 'Reynolds is dead. Somebody killed him in Vegas. Shot him.'

'You think it was Scaffazza?'

'Maybe, but a friend of mine is on the hook for it. I'd like to make sure he doesn't hang for it.'

'Whataya want me to do, Frankie?'

'I'd like to find Scaffazza,' Frank said.

'Frank, no offense,' Roselli said, 'Scaffazza's a hard guy. I wouldn't want you to get hurt. You got somebody can back you up?'

'Not here, but I got somebody in Vegas. I could get him here...'

'I tell you what,' Roselli said, 'I'm gonna help you, because I don't like that scumbag. You go back to Vegas. I'm gonna have somebody bring him to you.'

'Alive, Johnny?'

'Of course alive. *Che cazzo*, what the fuck I look like to you, some mad dog killer?'

'No, Johnny,' Frank said, hurriedly, 'I didn't mean—'

'Forget it,' Roselli said. 'Consider this a gift, from me to you, Frank. I'll bring him to you. Where you gonna be?'

'The Sands.'

'I'll call you when I set it up. *Ve bene*?'

'*Va bene*,' Frank agreed. 'All right.'

'Now, let's get the check—'

'It's on me, Johnny,' Frank said. 'I invited you.'

'*Bene*,' Roselli said. 'Thank you, Frank. I gotta go, but I'll call you, eh?'

'Thanks, Johnny.'

The two men shook hands and Roselli left. When the waiter came with the check Frank asked, 'Can you bring me a phone? Thanks.'

FORTY-NINE

The conversation between Frank and Johnny Roselli took place while Elvis and I were in Laughlin.

Laughlin was a small town nobody knew about until a guy named Don Laughlin decided to build a casino and motel. The Riverside Resort and Casino had twelve slots, two tables, .98 cent chicken dinners, and eight rooms, of which four were available for rent. Laughlin and his family lived in the other four. Laughlin actually got to name the town himself when the US Postal Service asked him to do so.

The place was always busy. Laughlin saw a great potential for tourism in the town, but it hadn't happened yet. The place was located in the southernmost tip of Nevada, right on the Colorado River, where the state came together with Arizona, so maybe he was right and it would grow. Time would tell.

Danny had tracked down a guy named Ed Rosette who actually lived across the river in Bullhead City, Arizona. But he currently worked at the Riverside. What better way to hide the fact that he'd embezzled millions of dollars than to move somewhere and get a job?

If Rosette thought Danny might discover that he was really Albert Kroner, successfully framing him for murder would have been a great way to get rid of him. But Elvis came up with a good question as we drove into Bullhead City.

'If this feller Rosette killed Reynolds to frame Danny,' he asked, 'why not just kill Danny?'

Out of the mouths of babes, and kings of rock 'n roll.

Rosette had a house in Bullhead City. He wasn't there, but he also had a very helpful neighbor.

'Lookin' for Ed?' he asked. He was putting out his garbage.

'That's right.'

'You'll find him at work right now,' the man said. He put his garbage can down, then placed his hands on his hips and regarded us. 'The Riverside Casino. He'll be working til around midnight tonight.'

'Thanks,' I said. 'You're very helpful.'

'We're neighbors,' the man said. 'We try to look out for each other. When Ed's not around I keep an eye on his house. Same thing when I'm away.'

'How long have you been neighbors?'

'Oh, I guess Ed moved in a few months ago.'

That was within the time frame we were working with.

'Well, thanks very much.' We started back to the car.

'Want me to tell him you were here?' the man asked.

'That's OK,' I called back. 'We'll find him at the Riverside.'

We got in the car and headed for Laughlin.

We could see the Riverside from Bullhead City, but had to drive around the river to get there. We could have looked for a boat to cross over with, but I wanted to have the car available to us. Besides, if he was working til midnight we had time.

'We ain't drivin' back to Vegas tonight, are we?' Elvis asked.

'No,' I said. 'Even if we find Rosette we've got to figure out how to approach him. We won't have time to drive back tonight.'

'What if we can't find out if he's Albert Kroner? What do we do then?'

'I don't know, Elvis,' I said. 'I'm still thinking about that.'

We pulled into the parking lot in front of the Riverside.

'What about stayin' here?' he asked as we got out of the car.

I explained about the four hotel rooms and said, 'I'm sure they save them for their best customers.'

'Yeah, but you're from Vegas,' Elvis said. 'The Sands. What about professional courtesy?'

'I guess that's a possibility,' I said. Laughlin used to have a casino in Vegas until he sold it some years back. But if I remembered correctly, Laughlin didn't get along real well with Jack Entratter. He'd kept the mob out of his place, which had been called the 101 Club.

'Let's just see if we can locate Rosette and talk to him,' I said.

As we entered the casino Elvis said, 'We don't know what he does here.'

'Shouldn't be too hard to find out,' I said. 'If he's dealing there's only two tables. If he works on the slots, there are only twelve of them.'

Of course, there was a lounge and bar, a restaurant, and the motel. It wasn't as easy as it sounded.

Unless we asked somebody.

FIFTY

While Frank was in LA and we were in Laughlin, Dino got off the helicopter in Lake Tahoe, looking for a man named John Golffe. 'I've gotta take that one,' said golf player Dino.

A limo met him at the airport and took him to Harrah's, where he had taken a room. Dino's job was harder than Frank's – who only had to call Johnny Roselli to get a meeting – and mine. Tahoe was a bigger town than Laughlin.

Dean got to his room and broke out a Lake Tahoe phone book. He was surprised to find a phone number and address for John Golffe. He couldn't believe his luck. After all, how many John Golffe's could there be?

He went out to the limo and gave the driver the address. When they arrived, Dean looked at the house and decided that John Golffe couldn't be Albert Kroner. Who would be stupid enough to embezzle millions, and then build a mansion like this, right on the lake?

Dino had decided to take the direct approach. Rather than wear a hat and sunglasses like Elvis to go unnoticed, he strode to the front door looking like a resplendent Dean Martin, and rang the bell.

The tall man in his forties who opened the door, stared when he saw who was standing there and stammered, 'D-Dean M-Martin?'

'Are you John Golffe?' Dean asked the man.

'I - I am,' the man said. 'Y-you know who I am?'

'Mr Golffe,' Dean said, 'if it's OK with you, I'd like to come in and talk to you.'

'Well ... well, sure, Mr Martin,' the man said. 'C-come right in. C-can I get you a drink?'

Dean crossed the threshold and said, 'Coffee would be great.'

At the same time Jerry was tailing a man named Howard Cantrell. He was in his forties, tall and heavier than Albert Kroner supposedly was, but it was an easy thing to gain weight to try to change your appearance.

Jerry had decided not to use the direct approach, because Jerry's idea of direct could get out of hand. He'd save that for later. Instead, he just tailed the man for a while.

This fella Cantrell wasn't down on his luck, but he was pretty close. He lived in a downtown flophouse and dressed like he shopped at the Salvation Army. It was the perfect disguise for an embezzler. Jerry didn't know exactly what Dean and I were finding our guys doing, but he was willing to put his money on Howard Cantrell.

Elvis and I had a drink in the lounge. The King of Rock 'n Roll was eyeing the '98 cent Chicken Dinner' sign when I asked the bartender for the manager.

'We have a kitchen manager, a bar manager, motel manager, a—'

'I want whoever manages the whole shebang,' I said. 'Or Mr Laughlin, himself.'

'The boss?' the bartender said. 'Oh, he ain't here. But Mr Hassett runs the daily operations of the casino.'

'Then let's start there,' I said. 'I'd like to talk to Mr Hassett.'

'And who can I say is askin' for him?' the bartender wanted to know.

'My name is Eddie Gianelli,' I said. 'I'm here from the Sands in Vegas.'

Elvis had convinced me to go ahead and say who I was and where I was from. 'Might open some doors,' he offered.

'You know,' I said to him, 'I might start lettin' you call all the shots.'

Elvis was still studying the 98 cents sign.

'The Sands?' the bartender said, bucking up. 'The big time. Hey, you need a good bartender?'

'I might,' I said. 'If I get to talk to Mr Hassett.'

'I can do more than just serve beers, you know,' the man said. 'Look, my name's Connie Morton.'

'Connie?' Elvis said.

'Well,' Morton said, 'actually it's Conrad, but...' He shrugged and Elvis went back to examining the sign. 'Look, Mr Gianelli, lemme make you somethin'. I can whip up—'

'You know what Frank Sinatra drinks?' I asked him.

He straightened up to attention and said, 'Martini.'

'OK,' I said, 'get me Mr Hassett and make me a Martini, and we'll see.'

'All right!' Morton said. 'But, look, don't tell Mr Hassett—'

'I've got other things to discuss with Mr Hassett—' I started to say, and then stopped. 'OK, let's try this. Make me a Martini ... and point me in the direction of a guy named Ed Rosette.'

'Ed?'

'That's right.'

'Oh,' Morton said, 'you won't find Mr Rosette in here.'

'I won't?'

'No sir.'

'Why not?'

'He don't work in here.'

'I was told he worked at the Riverside.'

'But not in the casino,' Morton said. 'He works outside.'

'Outside?'

'The motel,' Morton said. 'He works in the motel.'

'Doing what?'

'Caretaker.'

'Care ... you mean he's the janitor?'

'They call him a caretaker,' Morton said. 'He handles everything inside and outside the motel.'

'Everything?'

'You know, cleaning, repairing, gardening.'

'What does he repair?' I asked.

'Whatever needs fixing. The guy's an electrical genius, among other things. He can fix anything.'

Albert Kroner had been a lawyer, not a Mr Fix-It.

'Connie,' I said, 'you better fix me that Martini.'

'Vodka or gin?'

'Vodka.'

'Olive or onion?'

'Olive.'

'And I'll have one of those, son,' Elvis said, pointing to the '98 cent Chicken Dinner' sign.

FIFTY-ONE

When Elvis got his chicken dinner it looked so good I ordered one for myself.

'We gonna talk to this Rosette fella?'

'Well,' I said, 'we're here, we might as well talk to him, but there's nothing in Danny's report about Kroner being anything but a lawyer.'

'Maybe he fixed things around the house.'

'Connie says he's an electrical genius.'

'What does Connie know?' Elvis asked. 'He's a bartender.'

Connie brought over a chicken dinner for me, and a Martini, which he set down with a flourish. He then stood there and regarded it proudly.

I lifted the icy glass and sipped it. Martinis weren't my drink, but as Martinis went, it wasn't bad. In fact, it was pretty good.

'Not bad, Connie,' I said.

Elvis pushed his plate of bones away and asked, 'Can I have another of these?'

I'd finished my Martini by the time Connie brought Elvis his second chicken dinner, so I asked for a beer.

'So, whataya think?' Connie asked, as he set it down.

'About what?'

'My Martini,' he said. 'Think I can work at the Sands?'

He looked so damn eager. I took my business card out and passed it to him.

'You come to Vegas and ask for me,' I said. 'We'll give you a try out. But understand, I don't hire the bartenders. That's somebody else's job. But I'll put in a good word for you.'

'Goddamn!' he said, doing a little dance. 'Thanks, Mr Gianelli. Thanks a lot.'

Elvis picked up a chicken breast and said, 'You're a nice guy, Eddie.'

'Yeah, yeah,' I said, 'let's finish eating and go and find Ed Rosette.'

'A lawyer?' John Golffe said.

'That's right,' Dean said.

'I assure you, Mr Martin, I don't know anything about the law.'

Dean looked around the expensively furnished living room and sipped his coffee. There was a fireplace, with many photos on the mantle – family photos.

'What do you do, Mr Golffe?'

'Real estate,' Golffe said. 'I buy and sell – in fact, I'm about to put this house up for sale.'

'I see.'

'Can I ask why you're looking for this man?

This lawyer? What's his name?'

'Albert Kroner. A friend of mine needs to find him.'

'So Dean Martin comes to Lake Tahoe to do what? Act as a private eye?'

Dino perked up, smiled and said, 'Well, yeah, pally, I guess that's what I'm doin'.'

'Oh,' Golffe said. 'Well ... more coffee?'

Jerry followed Howard Cantrell home. All the man had done all day was hit bars. Jerry had the feeling Cantrell was a professional drunk, the kind who could consume alcohol all day, and still operate.

Jerry decided he knew how to handle people like this.

The direct approach, after all.

Elvis and I left the casino and walked over to the motel. There was no janitor or caretaker on the grounds at that moment, so we went inside.

There was a desk clerk who probably didn't have a lot to do, not with only four rooms to rent.

'Is Ed around?' I asked.

The clerk was a woman in her sixties who had a small black and white TV behind the desk with her. She was watching an old movie.

'Ed?'

'Ed Rosette,' I said. 'He's your janitor?'

'Oh, yeah,' she said, 'he's around, some-where.'

'Could you make an educated guess as to where, exactly?' I asked.

'Probably out back.'

'How do we get out back?'

'Go out and around,' she said, 'or go through.'

'Thanks.'

I decided we'd try to walk through the building to the back. We found a corridor that led past the rooms and to a back door. As we stepped outside we saw a bald man in his forties wearing a green short-sleeved shirt and green short pants that looked like a uniform – a janitor's uniform – washing out some garbage pails with a hose. Elvis and I exchanged a glance. Man, I thought, what a perfect disguise for a guy who didn't want anyone to know he had millions of dollars in ill-gotten gains.

FIFTY-TWO

Over coffee John Golffe did his best to convince Dean Martin that he was not Albert Kroner.

'You can check my bona fides,' he said. 'I can give you references. I moved here from up north, Seattle, where I did most of my business.'

'Mr Golffe,' Dean said, 'I'll tell you the truth. I don't think you're Kroner, but I will ask you for a couple of references we can check out, just so we can cross you off the list.'

'That's fine,' Golffe said. 'I'll write them down for you.'

'And then,' Dean said, 'I want you to come to Vegas when I'm performing. I'll see that you get a free suite, and tickets to my show. How's that?'

'Well ... that would be great. Thank you.'

While the man went to write down the information, Dean finished his coffee, wishing he could have come up with something more helpful for Danny Bardini's case. He hoped the others were doing better than he was.

231

The guy ran.

As Jerry knocked on the door he heard the window open inside. He put his shoulder into the door and it cracked at the lock, slamming open. He saw Cantrell's trailing leg go out the window.

'Damn it,' he said.

He was used to guys running from him in Brooklyn. But now he was going to have to chase this guy through streets and back alleys he didn't know.

He leaned out the window, saw the guy going down a rickety fire escape. To his left he saw some of the bolts holding the metal to the building were loose. If he stepped out onto it, his weight would probably pull it loose.

He reached out, grabbed the fire escape with both hands, and pushed. With a sickening groan the rusty fire escape came loose from the building and fell. Cantrell was about halfway down from the fourth floor. The fire escape hit the ground with a loud crash. Jerry hoped the fall hadn't killed him.

He turned and rushed to get down there and see for himself.

Elvis looked at me and shrugged.

'Excuse me,' I said. I had to say it again before the man looked up at us. He was so bald he had no eyebrows, no sign of facial hair, at all. There was a big wet spot on the front of his shirt.

'Yeah?'

'Is your name Ed Rosette?'

'That's right,' Rosette said. 'If you got a problem, though, you gotta go through the clerk.'

'We're not guests.'

'Then I can't help ya.' He started to bend back to his task.

'I just need a moment of your time, sir,' I said.

'Eh?' he straightened up. 'What for?'

'Just to ask a few questions.'

Rosette frowned at me.

'Are you the police?'

'No,' I said, 'but I could call for one, if you like. Then you could answer his questions.'

'No,' he said, quickly. 'Don't do that. Ask your questions.'

'Have you ever heard of a man named Kroner, Albert Kroner?'

'Kroner?' Rosette repeated. 'Was he a guest here?'

'Not that I know of.'

'The name doesn't ring a bell,' Rosette said.

And it didn't register on his face, either. He looked annoyed, and he probably had something to hide since he didn't want me to call a cop, but I didn't think he was Kroner.

'Why are you looking for him?' Rosette asked. 'This Kroner?'

'Why does anyone look for someone?' I

233

asked. 'He's missing.'

'Well, I've never heard of him,' Rosette said. 'You can check with the clerk if you want to see if he was ever a guest.'

'Thanks,' I said.

'Can I go back to work now?'

'Sure,' I said. 'We don't want to keep you.'

Elvis and I went back into the hotel.

'D'ya think it's him?' he asked.

'No,' I said. 'What do you think?'

'He didn't seem to react when you said the name,' he commented.

'No, he didn't.'

'But if it is him,' Elvis said, 'won't he run now?'

'If he does, it would prove he was Kroner,' I said. 'No, whether it's him or not, I don't think he'll be leaving. He should still be here if we decide to come back.'

'But how will we know?' he asked.

I thought a moment, then said, 'We may have an inside man.'

'You want me to what?' Connie Morton asked.

'Call me if Ed Rosette quits his job,' I said. 'Or disappears.'

'What for?'

'I'm looking for a missing man,' I said. 'A man who doesn't want to be found. His name is Kroner. Sound familiar?'

Morton leaned on the bar and said, 'No, can't say it does.'

'Well, in order to stay missing he might have changed his name.'

'Ah,' Morton said, 'I get it. You think Ed might be Kroner.'

'I thought it, until I spoke to him,' I said, 'but just in case I'm wrong...'

'You want me to keep an eye on him.'

'Yes.'

'Will this help me get a job at the Sands?' he asked, hopefully.

'Oh yes,' I said, 'this will help you a lot.'

Morton straightened up and with a grin said, 'Then you can count on me.'

'Thanks, Connie.'

I took Elvis by the arm and led him outside.

'What are we gonna do now?'

'Head back to Vegas,' I said, 'but first I want to get to a phone.'

'To call who?'

'Kaminsky,' I said. 'I want to see if Danny got bailed out. If he didn't then I want to talk to him, too.'

'I bet Connie would let you use his phone.'

'No, I don't want anyone overhearing me,' I said. 'Let's find me a pay phone away from here.'

'Where?'

'We passed a gas station on the way into town,' I said. 'That'll do.'

FIFTY-THREE

Jerry found Howard Cantrell lying beneath the wreckage of the rusty fire escape. He was bleeding from a head wound, but was still alive.

Jerry grabbed two handfuls of fire escape and lifted it off the man. He tossed it aside with a racket.

'Oooh,' Cantrell moaned.

'Wake up!' Jerry said, prodding the man with his toe. 'You ain't dead ... yet.'

Cantrell opened his eyes and squinted up at Jerry.

'What happened?'

'The fire escape came loose from the building. You fell.'

'I coulda been killed.'

'That's what you get for running,' Jerry said. 'Why'd you do that?'

'I thought you was the cops.'

'What do you have to hide from the cops?'

'I don't need a reason to run when they don't need a reason to roust me.'

'Well, I ain't a cop,' Jerry said. 'I just wanna

ask you some questions. Come on, get up.'

Jerry put his hand out. Cantrell hesitated, then grabbed it and allowed the big man to pull him to his feet.

'Oh, ow,' he said, putting his hand to his back. 'Jeez, my back.'

'It ain't broke, or you wouldn't be standin',' Jerry said. 'Answer my questions and then you can go to a doctor, if you want.'

'No, no,' Cantrell said, 'it's just bruised. Whataya wanna ask me? Who are you, anyway?'

'Never mind,' Jerry said. 'Just answer my questions.'

Cantrell made a rude sound with his mouth and said, 'You sound like a cop.'

'Bite your tongue. You want a drink?'

'I could use one.'

'Well, come on,' Jerry said. 'I'll buy you one. Would a cop do that?'

Dean had the limo take him back to the Tahoe airport, and the helicopter back to Vegas. Playing detective may have been fun, but he'd accomplished little. He was worried about what I would think of his efforts to help.

He didn't realize that I would simply think he had done what I'd asked him to do, and thank him.

'They're trying to find a way to keep him inside,' Kaminsky told me.

237

'But you have the bail money.'

'Apparently, they didn't think we'd be able to raise the bond,' Kaminsky said. 'That we did has surprised them.'

'What can you do?'

'What Kaminsky usually does,' he said. 'Don't worry, I'll get him out. It'll just take more time. Meanwhile, what have you got for me?'

'Not much, yet,' I said. 'I'm working on Danny's active case, trying to find a man he was looking for. I'm thinking he might have done the murder and framed Danny to get him off his trail.'

'Is what he has to hide worth murder?' Kaminsky asked.

'A couple of million dollars that's not rightfully his.'

'That sounds like it's worth murder,' Kaminsky said. 'OK, keep at it, bubula. Kaminsky's counting on you.'

I hung up thinking, yeah, so is Danny.

It was just under a hundred miles back to Vegas. We would've gotten back before dark but Elvis wanted to stop and eat.

'You had two ninety-eight cent chicken dinners,' I reminded him.

'They were small,' he said. 'Come on, son. Don't tell me you're not a little hungry?'

'I could eat,' I admitted.

It almost felt like travelling with Jerry.

We stopped in a diner along the way, ate and got back on the road.

'When are you supposed to perform?' I asked.

'Tomorrow night.'

'Don't you have to rehearse?' I asked. 'Am I keeping you from—'

'My guys have to rehearse,' Elvis said. He took the hat and glasses off, ran his fingers through his mass of dark hair. 'I know my part, don't I?'

'I guess so,' I said. 'If you don't, who does?'

'I suppose this case you're workin' on will keep you from comin' to my show?'

'Probably,' I said. 'Besides, Frank's gonna be there. Why, do you need me?'

'I'll leave a ticket for you at the box office,' he said. 'Two, in case you want to bring somebody.'

'OK,' I said. 'Thanks.'

'Eddie,' he said, 'tell me about you and Danny.'

'We grew up in the same neighborhood in Brooklyn,' I said. 'Him, me and my brother. They were friends, really. I became friends with him after my brother was killed.'

'Older or younger.'

'Older,' I said. 'I looked up to him. After he died my family – well, it kind of got ripped apart. My father went crazy, I think, and my mother couldn't get over it.'

'Did they stay together, your parents?'

239

'They did, but pretty much lived separate lives. She died last year.'

'I'm sorry. I know what it's like to lose your mama.'

'Unlike you, I hadn't seen her for a while,' I said. 'I went back to Brooklyn for the funeral, but that was a bad idea. My family, what's left – my father, my sister – have no use for me.'

'That's too bad,' he said. 'My dad, Vernon, lives at Graceland with me. He takes care of my correspondence.'

'It's nice to have your dad working with you.'

'Yeah,' he said, 'we keep an eye on each other.'

'What about Red, Sonny and the others?'

'I like havin' them around,' Elvis said.

'I think Red would do anything for you.'

'He's been protecting me since high school,' Elvis said.

'How did that happen?'

'A few boys cornered me in the boys' bathroom one day. They were making fun of my hair, said they was gonna cut it. Red took it upon himself to step in. He kicked their asses, and we been friends from that day on.'

'Still lookin' out for you, from what I can see,' I said. 'He doesn't like me, much.'

'Give him time,' Elvis said. 'When he sees you don't want anythin' from me, he'll change his mind.'

'What do you think they've been doin' while

240

you've been with me?' I asked.

'What they usually do,' Elvis said. 'Gettin' in trouble. They're good ol' boys, they don't mean no harm. But they do get rowdy, sometimes.'

'Well,' I said, 'when we get back you can check on them. I'll check in with Jerry and Dean, see what they've found.'

'And Frank?' he said. 'You think he'll be back from LA? I'd like to hear about his meeting with Johnny Roselli.'

'So would I,' I said.

FIFTY-FOUR

When we got back to Vegas I dropped Elvis at the Riviera, promised to let him know what was going on. From there I drove to the Sands, where I intended to look for Jerry, Frank, Dean, or any combination of the three.

I found Jerry first.

'Mr G.!'

I turned, saw him coming across the lobby toward me.

'I was looking for you,' I said.

'And I was lookin' for you,' he said. 'When did you get back?'

'Just now. Did you talk to your man, Cantrell?'

'I did. What about you?'

'Yeah, we found Ed Rosette in Laughlin,' I said. 'Let's get a drink and exchange information. Then I'll call Dino and Frank and see what they've got.'

'Oh, yeah,' he said, 'Mr S. went to LA to see Johnny Roselli. I wanna hear about that.'

'You know Roselli?' I asked.

'I seen him,' he said, 'but I wouldn't say I

know him.'

'Come on,' I said, 'I'll buy you a beer...'

I didn't take Jerry to the bar in the casino, but to a special VIP lounge we have for high rollers. Luckily, no one was in there at the time except for a single bartender. I didn't want our conversation to be overheard by anyone.

I got two beers from the bartender, then we sat at one of the tables furthest away from the bar.

'OK, why don't you give me your story first,' I suggested.

'Sure thing, Mr G.,' he said. 'My guy's name was Howard Cantrell. He lives in a flophouse, does nothing but drink all day, and I don't think he's Albert Kroner. The only thing I found suspicious about him, was that he got nervous when I mentioned the cops.'

'Why'd you mention the cops?'

'He brought 'em up first,' Jerry said. 'Said I sounded like a cop.'

'You don't sound like any cop I ever met.'

'Right? Damn it, what a thing to say to me, huh? Anyway, I took him for a drink and tried to find out more about him. Turns out he's a pickpocket, which is why he spends so much time in bars and doesn't want anything to do with cops.'

'A pickpocket living in a flophouse would be a great cover for someone who embezzled two million dollars.'

'Yeah, it would,' Jerry said, 'but I don't think it's him. What about your guy?'

'My guy was Ed Rosette,' I said. 'He has a house in Bullhead City, Arizona, but he works across the lake in Laughlin, Nevada at the Riverside Casino Resort.'

'Is he a dealer?'

'That's what I thought we were gonna find,' I said, 'either a dealer or a bartender, but it turns out he's the janitor at the motel. He's also a Mr Fix-It around there, can repair anything, especially anything electrical.'

'Well, a janitor, that'd be a good cover for somebody who don't want people to know he's got millions. But do we know if our Mr Kroner knows anything about fixin' stuff?'

'No,' I said, 'we don't. I want to talk to Danny about it, but he's still inside.'

'I thought he was gettin' bailed out?'

'The cops, the DA and the judge are playin' fast and loose with the law,' I said, 'but Kaminsky is still tryin'. Meanwhile, I don't think Ed Rosette's the guy.'

'So, who does that leave?'

'Dean's guy, John Golffe.'

'Is he back?'

'I'm about to find out,' I said. I waved at the bartender and made motions for a phone. He brought it over and plugged it in beneath the table. I dialed Dean's suite and he picked up.

'Yeah, pally, I got back early,' he said. 'Where are you?'

'Jerry and me are in the VIP lounge,' I said. 'Why don't you come down and join us? Is Frank back?'

'I think so. You want me to bring him?'

'No, you come down first, and then we'll call Frank.'

'I'll be right there.'

I hung up, kept the phone on the table so I could call Frank later.

'How did it go with Elvis?' Jerry asked when I hung up.

'You know,' I said, 'bein' with him is almost like bein' with you.'

'I'll take that as a compliment, even though I can't carry a tune.'

'It's the eating,' I said. 'We were in the Riverside and they had ninety-eight cent chicken dinners. He had two while we were there, and then he wanted to eat again on the way back.'

'And what's the weird part of that?' he asked.

FIFTY-FIVE

We had fresh beers on the table when Dean arrived, casually dressed in tan slacks, an open collar polo shirt and loafers. He had a cigarette between the first and second fingers of his right hand. The bartender's eyes went wide when he walked in.

'What can I get you, Mr Martin?' he asked.

'Just bring me a club soda, pally,' Dean said. 'It's gettin' late.'

Dean sat down with us and the bartender brought him his soda.

'I hope you fellas had better luck than I did,' he said, 'because there's no way my guy is Albert Kroner.'

Jerry and I remained quiet.

'Well, I can see that's not good news,' Dean said.

I told him about Jerry's and my experiences with our guys, and how we had already decided it wasn't them.

'OK,' Dino said, 'so what are the chances that Danny got it wrong and it's not one of those three?'

'I suppose that's possible,' I said. 'I won't know until I can talk to him.'

'He's still inside?' Dean asked.

'Yeah, they're playin' games with the bail. Kaminsky's workin' on it.'

'If you want a different, more high-profile lawyer I can make some calls,' Dean said.

'I appreciate it, Dino, but not yet. Danny trusts Kaminsky.'

'OK, but the offer is out there,' Dean said. 'I don't feel I got the job done in Tahoe, so I'd still like to help.'

'Hey,' I said, 'you did what you said you'd do. I couldn't ask for more.'

'OK,' Dean said, 'so what about Frank and Johnny Roselli?'

'That's next,' I said, 'and I thought we'd all like to hear it, so I'm gonna ask Frank to come down here.'

Jerry and Dean nodded and talked between themselves as I dialed the phone.

'Frank?' I said, when he answered. 'I'm in the VIP lounge with Jerry and Dino. You wanna join us?'

Frank came down, dressed as casually as Dino was. He sat with us and had the bartender bring him a Martini.

'How'd you boys all make out?' he asked, and listened patiently to our stories.

'Where's the king?' he asked, with only the slightest hint of irony in his tone.

'I dropped him at his hotel,' I said. 'He's got to connect with his people, and he has a show to do tomorrow night.'

'We're all goin', right?' Frank asked.

'Definitely,' Dean said.

'Yeah, Jerry and I are goin',' I said.

'We are?' Jerry asked.

'Elvis is leavin' two tickets at the box office for us.'

'That's great.'

'Frank?' I said. 'How did things go with Johnny Roselli?'

'We had a nice lunch, danced around each other for a while before we got down to business.'

'Did he know Reynolds?'

'He says no,' Frank replied, 'but he knew Scaffazza. Had nothin' good to say about him, called him names and said he fired him.'

'I thought "fired" meant "dead" in those circles,' I said.

'That was the old Mafia,' Dean said. 'This is the new Mafia.'

'Johnny would've killed him if he could get away with it,' Frank said. 'I mean, if he really felt the way he was tellin' me.'

'Do you think he was coverin' for the guy?' Jerry asked.

'You know, I might think that,' Frank said, 'but for one thing.'

'What's that?' Dean asked.

'He says he's gonna deliver Scaffazza to us

here, so we can talk to him.'

'"Deliver"?' Jerry said. 'Now that does sound like dead.'

'In the desert dead,' Dino agreed.

'Well, he's supposed to call and tell me where we can meet Scaffazza.'

'Maybe he's gonna let Scaffazza talk to us and then kill 'im,' Jerry said.

'I don't mean to sound crass, but as long as we get to talk to him, I don't really care what happens to him afterward.'

'Atta boy, Mr G.,' Jerry said. 'You're learnin'.'

FIFTY-SIX

We left the VIP lounge like four fighters going back to their own corners. Frank was the only one who seemed to have scored some points. With Dean, Jerry and I all thinking that our guy was not Albert Kroner, we were back where we started. Frank was the only one who had made some progress.

Maybe.

It depended on how true to his word Johnny Roselli was. We wouldn't know that until he called Frank and came through with a meet with Joey Scaffazza.

I went out to my own car and drove home to get a good night's sleep.

Or so I thought.

In the middle of the night there was a pounding on my door. Worried that it might be Jerry, or have something to do with Danny, I ran to the door wearing only pajama bottoms.

When I opened the door it wasn't Jerry, or Kaminsky, but two guys wearing black suits. They stood with their hands clasped in front of them.

'Eddie Gianelli?' one of them asked.

'That's right.'

'Answer your phone.'

'What?'

The phone rang. He nodded toward it and said, 'Answer it.'

I kept my eyes on them while I moved to the phone and picked it up.

'Hello?'

'Go with them.'

'Frank?'

'Yeah, it's me,' Frank said. 'Go with them, Eddie. It's OK.'

'Yeah, but...' He hung up before I could ask anything else. I hung up and looked at the two men at the door.

'OK?' the spokesman asked.

'Just let me put something on.'

'Go ahead.'

I went back to my bedroom to get dressed. I thought about going out the window, and might have if Frank hadn't called. Instead I put on jeans, a T-shirt, a windbreaker and a pair of sneakers.

'OK,' I said, at the door. I started to think of them as Number One (the spokesman) and Number Two. 'Do I follow you, or—'

'We'll take you,' Number One said, 'and bring you back.'

'Fine,' I said. 'Let's go.'

I followed them to a black sedan parked in

front of the house. They both got in front, and I got in the back. No restraints, no blindfold, and the doors were not locked. There didn't seem to be anything to worry about.

Yet.

The windows were tinted dark, so it was hard for me to see where we were going. I could see out the front windshield, but their heads were in the way and I wasn't picking up much that would help me.

Finally, the car stopped and the driver – Number Two – turned off the engine.

'We're here,' Number One said.

'Where, exactly?' I asked.

'Here,' was all he said. 'You can get out.'

They got out, so I had no choice but to follow. I closed the back door behind me and looked at the house we were in front of. It was a large, wood-framed house, two stories, not a mansion, but way beyond my means.

'This way,' Number One said.

I followed them up the walk, which was encouraging. If they had been taking me somewhere, one of them would have been in front of me and one behind.

We didn't go to the front, but to a side door that was a few steps down. Number Two used a key to enter, and I followed them in. He turned on a light and I saw three steps going down.

'Down there,' Number Two said.

'By myself?'

'We'll be waitin' here,' he promised, 'to take

you back.'

I hesitated, then shrugged and said, 'OK.'

I went down the stairs, found myself in what, for want of a better word, I'll call a rec room. Tiled floor, wood-paneled walls, a bar against one wall. In the center was a table with four chairs. Seated at the table, eating, was an older man wearing dark glasses. He was working on something with a knife and fork. He cut it, put a piece in his mouth, and then looked up at me.

'*Scungilli*,' Sam Giancana said to me. 'You want some, Eddie?'

FIFTY-SEVEN

'I'm not a snail guy, Momo,' I said, then, thinking better of it, I said, 'Mr Giancana.'

'No, no,' he said, 'you can call me Momo. Come, sit. Have some wine, at least.'

I walked to the table and sat across from him. I may not have liked snails, but the marinara sauce it had been prepared in smelled good. He poured me a glass of red wine, then picked up his knife and fork.

'I had this brought in from the Bootlegger restaurant,' Giancana said. 'Frank always spoke very highly of it. It's not as good as what we have in Chicago, but eh! It will do.' He put another bite into his mouth. His suit jacket was draped over the back of his chair. He had a cloth napkin around his neck so he wouldn't get sauce on his white shirt.

I drank some wine.

'I'm sorry to wake you up, Eddie, but we needed to talk,' he said.

'About what?' I asked.

'Joey Scaffazza.'

'What about him?'

'He's one of mine.'

'Scaffazza works for you? Inside Roselli's organization?'

Momo nodded.

'Ever since '56, when Johnny took over our operations in Vegas, I've had someone inside. For the past couple of years it's been Scaffazza.'

Roselli ran the Mafia's operation in Vegas, making sure they got their skim from the various casinos they owned, but he did it from LA. Ostensibly, as far as the government was concerned, Johnny was employed as a producer for Monogram Studios. It was Roselli who 'convinced' Columbia Pictures President Harry Cohn to sign Marilyn Monroe to a contract in 1948, on the orders of his boss Tony Arcardo. Other than that, Johnny's contribution to Hollywood was to sleep with as many starlets as he could.

'Why are you telling me this?' I asked.

He looked at me, and gestured with his knife, which he held in his right hand, European style.

'Because I heard that you wanna talk to Scaffazza about some problem you got here in Vegas,' he said. 'I heard that Johnny promised to deliver Scaffazza to Frank.'

'Alive.'

'Yeah, alive,' Giancana said. 'I heard that, too. Lately, Johnny ain't so happy with Joey, but that's OK. I already got another man inside.

So if Johnny snuffs Joey...' He shrugged.

'Then if you don't care if Johnny kills Joey, why bring me here?'

'I want you to know you're dealin' with one of my people,' Giancana said.

'Do you want me to tell you why?'

He put another piece of *scungilli* in his mouth and said, 'Nah. Frankie already explained.'

'Then I'm still confused as to why I'm here,' I said. 'Other than the snails and wine.'

'We got-a more sauce,' he said, 'and some pasta. You want some-a dat?' I noticed that Giancana's Italian accent always got heavier when he talked about food. I'd noticed it the other couple of times I'd been ushered into his presence. Seemed to me he was always eating when we talked. Or drinking wine. Or both.

'No, thanks,' I said. 'When I get back home I'm goin' back to bed.'

'Suit yourself.' He cut another piece and forked it into his mouth, then pointed at me with the fork, this time. 'If Johnny kills Scaffazza, that's one thing. But if somebody outside the organization kills him – a civilian – that ain't OK. Do I make myself clear?'

'Wait,' I said, 'you think I want to kill Scaffazza?'

Momo shrugged.

'Momo, I don't kill people.'

'Jerry does. He's good at it.'

I think, since I had met Jerry, that might have been the first time anybody actually said he killed people.

'Well, he's not going to kill Scaffazza,' I assured him. 'That's not what I'm after.'

'Good,' Momo said, picking up his wine glass, 'good, I'm glad to hear that, Eddie.'

'But I do need to talk to Scaffazza,' I said. 'And I might need Jerry to convince him to talk to me.'

'Well,' Giancana said, 'that big Hebe is a good convincer, too.'

'Yes,' I said, 'he is. Can I ask you a question?'

'Sure, go ahead. After all, I dragged you out of a warm bed, didn't I?' He leaned forward. 'Didn't have a broad there with you, did ya? One of them leggy Vegas showgirls?'

'No,' I said, thinking about Valerie, 'not tonight.'

'Huh, too bad.' He went back to his food. 'OK, so what's your question?'

'Do you know a guy named William Reynolds?' I asked. 'Did you ever know him?'

'Reynolds,' Momo said, 'Not Italian.'

'No.'

'Not that I only know Italians,' Momo said, 'even though most of my friends are Italian. But ... no, I never hearda the bum. Why?'

'Somebody killed him here in town.'

'Ah, Frankie tol' me somebody got killed,' Momo said. 'He didn't tell me the name. Reynolds, huh?'

'That's right.'

257

'Vinnie!' he shouted.

I heard footsteps, and then Number One appeared and said, 'Yes, Mr Giancana?'

'We know a guy named Reynolds?' He looked at me.

'William,' I said.

'William Reynolds.'

'Or Billy,' I said.

Vinnie cocked his head, like he was thinking it over, then said, 'No, sir, don't know 'im.'

Giancana looked at me. 'Good enough?'

'Good enough. Thanks.'

'Vinnie,' he said, 'take Eddie home.'

'Yes, sir.'

I stood up, was about to say something else to the mob boss, but he had already turned his attention back to his *scungilli* and forgot I was there.

I followed Vinnie up the stairs...

They pulled the car to the curb in front of my house.

'Thanks for the ride, boys.'

Vinnie turned around.

'About Joey Scaffazza.'

'Yeah?'

Number Two kept his eyes front.

'He's a scumbag,' he said, 'but he's a smart scumbag. He plays both ends against the middle, if you get my drift.'

'I think I do.'

'If he was to end up dead, nobody would

miss 'im,' Vinnie said. 'Just don't let him pull a fast one on you.'

'I understand.'

'Goodnight, Mr Gianelli.'

'Goodnight, Vinnie.'

I got out and the car pulled away from the curb quietly, so as not to annoy my neighbors.

I went back to bed.

FIFTY-EIGHT

In the morning I replayed over the scene with Giancana in my head over coffee and toast. It was almost like a dream, except I could still smell the marinara and taste the red wine.

Giancana actually thought he had to warn me against killing one of his men. When exactly did I get that kind of reputation? Was I fooling myself all these years thinking I wasn't mobbed up when people like Hargrove and Giancana obviously thought I was? Or considered that I was?

And Jerry ... I had started to think of Jerry as this lovable leg-breaker. Despite his ever present .45, I never really thought of him as a killer. Not even when he killed somebody to save my life. But to Sam Giancana, that's what he was, a killer – and somebody who was good at it.

But maybe it wasn't the time for me to re-examine my life, and my friendships. Danny was still in jail on a murder charge, depending on me to get him out and prove him innocent.

I got mad, though, driving to the Sands, and when I arrived there I stormed up to Frank's suite and pounded on his door.

'Eddie!' he said, when he opened the door. Although dressed in slacks and a button-down white shirt, the shirt was not yet tucked in and his hair hadn't been combed.

'Surprised to see me, Frank?' I demanded. 'Did you think I'd be dead?'

'What? Dead? No, of course not...'

I stormed past him into the suite. He closed the door, turned to face me.

'Wait a minute,' he said, holding his hands up in a placating gesture. 'Let me explain.'

'That's exactly what I want, Frank,' I said, 'an explanation. Why did you serve me up to Sam Giancana?'

'I didn't serve you up to anybody,' Frank insisted. 'Look, sit down, have some coffee, relax, Eddie. I can explain.'

I took a deep breath and realized what I was doing. This could get me fired. As much as Jack Entratter might like me, he'd never stand for me talking this way to Frank Sinatra.

There was a silver coffee pot on the coffee table with several china cups. I walked over, sat down, and filled one for myself. When I saw that he had not had a cup yet, I filled one for him, too.

He came over, sat across from me in an armchair, and picked up the cup.

'Thanks. Look, I got a call from Momo last night. He knew all about my meeting with Roselli, and about Joey Scaffazza. He told me he

261

was coming to Vegas and wanted to talk to you. Just talk. He said he'd send two guys to your house to escort you to him and that I should make sure you went with them.' He sipped his coffee again, sat back in his chair. 'Eddie, you don't tell Sam Giancana no. But I made sure that all he wanted to do with you was talk.'

'Do you know what he wanted to talk about? Specifically?'

'No,' Frank said, 'he didn't tell me that.' He held his hand out to me. 'And it's totally up to you if you want to tell me. If it was a confidential conversation—'

'Nothing was said about keeping it confidential, Frank,' I said, and went on to relate the entire conversation to him.

'So Scaffazza is Momo's rat inside Roselli's organization?' Frank said. 'Wow.'

'Yeah.'

'But Momo okayed you talkin' to him?'

'He did,' I said, 'but he also told me not to kill him.'

Frank looked surprised.

'Why would he tell you that?'

'Obviously,' I said, 'Momo thinks I'm a killer.'

'B-but ... why? What have you ever done to make him think that?'

'Exactly!'

'All right,' Frank said, 'I can understand why you were so mad. I won't tell Jack Entratter how you treated me this morning.'

I hesitated, then said, 'Thank you.'

'I'm expecting Johnny to call me today,' he said. 'When you go talk to Scaffazza I want to come along.'

'Why?'

'Let's just say I want to see this through. I got the meet, I want to go to it.'

'OK,' I said. 'I don't have a problem with that.'

After a moment he said, 'We, uh, will be takin' Jerry along, right?'

'Oh yeah,' I said.

We both drank our coffee.

FIFTY-NINE

After I left Frank I tried to call Kaminsky, but he didn't answer, and neither did his assistant. Of course, the phone number I had was for his office – his real office – and he was never there.

I called information and got the phone number for Grabstein's Deli. Then I called there and asked for Kaminsky.

'Who shall I say is calling?' Manny asked.

'Tell him it's Eddie G.'

'Hold on.'

After a few moments Kaminsky came on.

'Hey, bubula, what's going on?'

'I was about to ask you the same question. You get Danny out yet?'

'I'm meeting with the judge in his chambers later this morning,' he said. 'I should be able to get it done then.'

'Well, I need to talk to Danny as soon as I can,' I said.

'He's still in holding,' Kaminsky said. 'They will only move him if his bail is denied.'

'Is that a possibility?' I asked. 'That they'd

deny it after they approved it?'

'Anything's possible, bubby,' he said. 'But you can go down and see him. They'll let you in because you represent me.'

'Yeah, and they're supposed to let him out because we've got the bail money.'

'They're screwing around with that,' he said, 'but they wouldn't screw with Kaminsky seeing his own client – and you represent Kaminsky. Don't you forget that.'

'I won't.'

'I'll talk to you later.'

We hung up. I was using a phone in the lobby of the Sands, and Jerry was standing by.

'Let's go,' I said.

'Where?'

'To see Danny,' I said. 'I want to take everything we've learned and run it by him.'

'We ain't learned much,' Jerry observed.

'So it won't take that long.'

We got into the Caddy and drove down to the police station.

I got in to see Danny, but Jerry didn't.

'One at the time,' the cops told me.

Not sure if that was actually the rule, but I told Jerry, 'It's OK, wait out here.'

'Sure, Mr G.,' he said, 'I'll wait outside. Bein' in a police station gives me the willies, you know?'

'Yeah,' I said, 'I know.'

They took Danny out of his cell and put him

265

in a room so I could see him. He was seated at a table, handcuffed. He looked more rumpled and messed up than I'd ever seen him, and he had a welt over one eye.

'What's that from?'

'Fella wanted my bunk,' he said.

'Did he get it?'

'Whatayou think?'

I didn't think so. I sat down across from him.

'I don't know how much time I've got so I'll talk fast,' I said.

I told him we'd checked out all three men he suspected could be Kroner. I told him what we'd found out, and what Frank had done. I told him everybody who was helping.

'Jesus, Eddie,' he said, 'you got Frank Sinatra, Dean Martin and Elvis Presley workin' on this?'

'And me and Jerry.'

'Well, sure, I know that, but these other guys ... How'd you do that?'

'They all volunteered, Danny.'

'Or you volunteered them.'

'Nope, it was their own decision,' I said.

'Well,' Danny said, 'tell 'em all I appreciate it – especially Elvis. I mean, he was willing to put up two hundred grand for me.'

'You can tell them that when you get out.'

'Yeah,' he said, 'whenever that is.'

'Kaminsky says he's meeting with the judge today,' I said. 'In his chambers. He'll get you out.'

'Yeah, I know he will,' he agreed, but he didn't sound very convincing.

'What about this Scaffazza guy?' he asked. 'Think you can make a case for him killin' Reynolds instead of me?'

'I don't know,' I said. 'What would his motive be?'

'I don't know ... money?'

'Possibly. What about these three suspects of yours? What do you think of them?'

'I think one of them is Kroner.'

'I gotta tell you, Danny,' I said, 'that doesn't seem likely.'

'This kind of case is tricky, Eddie,' he said. 'If they all convinced you guys, I still think one of them is doin' a better job than the rest. One of them's gotta be him, but even if he is, there's no proof he had anything to do with the murder.'

'All we have to do is connect Reynolds to one of them,' I said. 'Look, Danny, I need a DMV contact.'

'What for?'

I told him how Hargrove had messed with the old lady's memory about the license plate she'd seen.

'That sonofabitch.'

'I want to run the plate the other three ways and see if we come up with somebody who looks like you.'

'You're a smart guy, Eddie,' he said. 'Yeah, we got a DMV guy. Talk to Penny, she'll give you the number. How's she holdin' up?'

'Like a trooper.'

'When do you think you'll be seein' this Scaffazza?'

'As soon as Frank gets the call,' I said, 'and he wants to go with me.'

'Well, you make sure you take Jerry with you.'

'We will.'

'Anything else?'

'Yeah,' I said, 'have you thought about another lawyer? The guys have sort of hinted they can get you somebody a little more high profile.'

'Kaminsky's my guy, Eddie,' he said. 'Don't worry, he'll get me out.'

'OK,' I said, 'if you trust him, so do I.'

'I trust him like I trust you.'

'Don't worry, Danny,' I said. 'We're all workin' on this for you.'

'I appreciate it,' he said, 'and look into those three guys a little deeper. I'd swear one of them is Kroner.'

'OK,' I said, 'I'll get my team back on the job.'

'Your team,' Danny said, with a lopsided grin. 'Some team.'

'I'll see you soon,' I said, 'on the outside.'

I started for the door, then stopped.

'What?' he asked.

'Your gun.'

'What about it?'

'The cops claim it's the murder weapon.'

'Impossible.'

'Is it your only gun?'

'No, I have one other. I keep it at home.'

'What kind?'

'A thirty-two.'

'Could someone have gotten ahold of your thirty-eight and killed Reynolds with it?'

'That would've been kinda hard.'

'Why?'

'Because I had my gun on me the day of the murder.'

'The whole time?'

'Yep.'

'Never put it down?'

'Nope.'

'Damn.'

He nodded. I left as a guard took him back to his cell.

SIXTY

Jerry was waiting out in front of the building, like he said.

'How's the Shamus?' he asked.

'Holdin' up,' I said. 'He's confident that Kaminsky can get him out.'

'So he don't want a new lawyer?'

'Nope.'

'Whatta we do now?'

'We go see Penny,' I said. 'She's going to hook us up with someone at the DMV to check those plate numbers.'

'Fremont Street?'

'Right.'

'Here's the number,' Penny said, turning her Rolodex around to face me, 'but why don't you let me call him, Eddie? He knows me? You won't need to explain so much.'

'OK, Penny,' I said, taking out the slip of paper with the numbers on it. 'Give him these and let's see what comes back.'

She sat down at her desk and dialed. I drifted into Danny's office, with Jerry behind me.

'So that's gettin' done,' he said. 'Now what?'

'Danny insists one of the three men we checked out is Kroner,' I said. 'I need more information about him.'

'From where? And who?'

'From Chicago,' I said, 'and I don't know who. Not yet. But we also have to address the question of the gun.'

'How do we do that?' Jerry asked.

Before I could answer, Penny came in and said, 'OK, our guy is working on the plate numbers.'

'Good,' I said. 'Penny, do you have a key to Danny's apartment?'

Her face colored slightly and she said, 'I don't, but there's an extra in his desk.'

She went around behind Danny's desk, opened the drawer and came out with two keys.

'The downstairs key, and his apartment door key,' she said.

'That's it?' I asked. 'That's all I'd need to get inside?'

'Yes?'

'Do you know what this key is for?' I asked. It was a third, smaller one.

'No.'

'Does he have any other keys?'

'Well, office keys, keys to his file cabinets and desk...'

'Any safety deposit box keys?'

'Not that I'm aware of.'

This one didn't look like a safety deposit box

271

key, but Jerry had another idea.

'What about gun safe keys?' Jerry asked.

'A gun safe?'

'A safe where he'd keep extra guns,' Jerry said. 'Does he have one of those?'

'I ... don't think so.'

'Penny,' I said, 'not that we don't believe you, but Jerry and I are going to search this place, and then Danny's apartment.'

'Why?'

'The cops insist that Danny's gun killed Reynolds.'

'That's impossible.'

'No,' I said, 'what's impossible is Danny killin' Reynolds when he says he didn't. That doesn't mean somebody else didn't kill him with Danny's gun.'

'But he told you he had it on him the whole day,' Jerry reminded me.

'I know,' I said. 'I just want to search to be thorough.'

'All right,' Penny said. 'I can help.'

'No,' I said. 'I want you to go home, Penny.'

'Why? I can help here, and then at Danny's apartment.'

'If it ever comes up that we searched Danny's place I want to be able to say you weren't there.'

'Why?'

'Because somebody – a cop, a lawyer, a jury – will have a hard time believing that you didn't cover up evidence for the man you love.'

Now she colored furiously.

'I never said—'

'I know,' I cut her off. 'I said it. Go home, Penny. I'll call you and let you know when we're done.'

'And what you find,' she said, 'if anything.'

'I promise.'

'OK,' she said. She went out to her desk and grabbed her purse. 'I'm going,' she called out.

I looked at Jerry. 'Make sure she goes out the door.'

'Right.'

He went into the outer office and walked Penny to the door, and out. Then he came back in.

'I think she's mad at me.'

'She'll get over it. Let's take a look around.'

'In here and out there?'

I hesitated, then said, 'Oh hell, sure. Let's go all the way. You take the outer, and I'll look in here.'

'And what are we lookin' for?'

'I don't know, Jerry,' I replied. 'Like I said, I'm just tryin' to be thorough.'

'Right, thorough.'

He went into the other room.

'Thorough,' I called out, after a few moments, 'but neat!'

SIXTY-ONE

The only thing that had anything to do with a gun was in a bottom drawer of Danny's desk. It was a kit he'd used to clean his weapon. Nothing but oils and cloths, and brushes.

Jerry came walking in and said, 'I got nothin'.'

'OK,' I said, 'me, neither.' I looked at him. 'That could be good or bad, right?'

'Right.'

'OK,' I said, 'let's go to his apartment.'

On the way down the stairs he asked, 'Can we get somethin' to eat on the way?'

'Sure,' I said, 'somethin' we can take along with us. Burger and fries?'

'And a shake?'

'And a shake.'

'Sure,' he agreed.

We hit the street and walked to the Caddy.

We entered Danny's place carrying a bag of burgers and fries.

'Let's eat it in his kitchen,' I said. 'I don't want to leave grease all over the place.'

'OK.'

We found two beers in his refrigerator to wash it all down with.

'Hey,' he said, 'we're gonna see Elvis perform tonight, huh?'

'I hope so.'

'What?'

'I just mean things have to go right for us to have time to go.'

'Mr S. and Dino will be there.'

I didn't respond.

'Mr G.?'

'Huh?'

'Whattsa matter?'

'I was just thinking that Frank might know somebody in Chicago we could use to run down information on Kroner.'

'Wanna give him a call?'

'Yeah,' I said, 'but let's have a look around first, huh?'

'Sure,' he said, taking his second burger out of the bag, 'as soon as we finish eatin'.'

We did a thorough search of Danny's apartment, just in case – for whatever reason – he hadn't told us, or Penny, about another gun.

Jerry and I examined the lock on his front door, and all his windows, to see if we could figure out if any of them had been forced.

'That's it,' I said, frustrated.

'Nothin' here, nothin' at the office.'

'Wait...'

'For what?'

'Danny told me he had another gun here,' I said. 'A thirty-two.'

'Where is it?'

I looked around, as if I'd see it just lying in the open.

'We missed it,' I said. 'He has a hidey-hole around here someplace.'

'Ask him.'

'I could do that,' I said, 'but we're smart, right?'

'You are,' Jerry said.

'Yeah, right,' I said. 'Come on, we can figure this out. False wall, loose floorboard, something. Come on, once more through.'

'OK,' he said, 'but let's switch.'

We had divvied up the apartment 50-50, so his idea to switch was good. One of us might find something the other one missed.

'Good idea.'

We went at it again.

'Mr G.?' Jerry called a short time later.

I walked into the kitchen, found him with several large bowls on the counter. I realized he had emptied all of Danny's cereal into the bowls. I hadn't done that.

'Did you find the gun?'

'No,' he said, 'but I found this.' He held up a brown envelope, sealed and rubber banded. From the shape of it, it wasn't hard to figure out the contents.

'Cash?' I said.

'Feels like it.'

'Put it back, Jerry.'

'Ain'tcha curious about how much it is?'

'Yes,' I said, 'but put it back. That's not what we're looking for.'

He shrugged, put it back in the cereal box, and then started pouring cereal back into the boxes from the bowls.

'You check the freezer?' I asked.

'No.'

'Neither did I.'

I opened the freezer and looked inside. Some frozen dinners, ice cubes, a bottle of vodka, and in the back a plastic baggie with a gun in it.

'Got it,' I said. I took it out and showed it to him.

'Has it been fired?'

'Don't know, but it doesn't matter,' I said. 'So far nobody's been shot with a thirty-two.'

'I'm curious.'

I handed it to him. He opened the baggie, took out the gun, smelled it, and replaced it.

'Ain't been fired.'

I put it back in the freezer.

He put the cereal boxes back in the cupboard.

'So, nothing,' he said, facing me.

'Nope. I checked his desk, here. Found his bills: phone, electric, credit cards, gym—'

'Wait, gym?'

'Yup. He works out.'

'Then he's got a locker there.'

'You're right,' I said. Yeah, I thought, I'm the smart one. 'Let's check that out.'

'You got the address?'

'I'll get it off the bill.'

I did that, and we left, driving directly to the gym Danny owed his well-toned muscles to.

SIXTY-TWO

Danny's gym was in a strip mall located half-way between his apartment and his office. Very handy. We went inside. I wondered if we were going to be allowed to search his locker.

A muscular, blond young man was manning the front desk. He was wearing some sort of Jack LaLanne looking leotard.

'Hi,' I said, 'is there a manager around I can talk to?'

He suddenly looked concerned.

'Is there a problem with your membership, sir?'

'I'm not a member,' I said. 'I just want to talk to the manager.'

'If you have a problem, I'm sure I can—'

'Get the manager,' Jerry growled.

The young man, fit and about six feet tall, took one look into Jerry's eyes and said, 'Yes, sir.'

As he walked away I turned and said to Jerry, 'You scared him.'

'I was tryin' to.'

'Bully,' I said, shaking my head.

The guy came back with a clone, another guy in a leotard, this one dark-haired. He too looked to be in his twenties.

'Hello, I'm Craig. Can I help you? Carl says you have a problem with your membership?'

'Carl's wrong, Craig,' I said. 'I told Carl I'm not a member.'

The manager looked past me to Jerry.

'I ain't a member, either,' Jerry said, 'and Carl's an idiot.'

'Now look here—' the manager said, but Jerry decided to take matters into his own hands – literally.

He stepped forward and grabbed hold of the man's right arm, just above the bicep and squeezed.

'We need to see the locker room,' he said, 'now!'

'Ow-wow,' the man said, getting up on his toes, 'OK, OK, this way.'

Jerry loosened his hold on the guy's arm, but didn't let go.

'Should I call the police?' Carl asked.

'If he does,' Jerry said to Craig, 'I'll tear your arm off.'

'No police, Carl,' Craig said. 'Just go back to work.'

'The locker room,' Jerry reminded him.

'Th-this way.'

He led us down a hall to a room full of lockers. There were a few guys, in various stages of dress and undress. One was pulling on a pair of shorts, another was wrapped in a towel. The third one had finished getting dressed and was on his way out.

'We need to know which locker is Danny Bardini's,' Jerry said.

'D-Danny?'

'Come on,' I said. 'Which one?'

'I-I dunno, I swear ... I'd have to look it up.'

'Is Danny in trouble?'

I turned. The speaker was the guy in the towel. He had good shoulders and upper arms, but needed to do some more sit-ups.

'He is,' I said. 'I need to look in his locker.'

'Who are you?'

'Eddie Gianelli.'

'Hey,' the guy said, 'Danny's mentioned you. I'm Dwayne Brewster. He's got the locker next to mine. Right here.' Brewster pointed.

'Thanks,' I said. I looked at Jerry. 'Keep ahold of our friend, here.'

'You got it.'

I took out Danny's key chain, hoping that the third key would open his locker. It did. I swung the door open and the smell of sweat wafted out. Danny needed to wash his gym shorts. The smell took me right back to my high school locker room.

There was a T-shirt, the offending shorts, a pair of sneakers, a couple of towels – also smelly – some deodorant, a comb, a tube of Brylcreem. No gun, but of course I wasn't looking for a gun. Danny had already turned it over to the cops. I was just looking for ... something helpful. Something to show me how easy it might have been for someone to take it from the locker, use it, and put it back.

'Anything?' Jerry asked.

'Nothing,' I said.

'What are you guys lookin' for?' Brewster asked.

'Somethin' to help Danny.'

'What's he need?'

'It's a little complicated.'

Brewster opened his own locker, reached in and brought out something shiny. It was a deputy sheriff's badge.

'Try me,' he said. 'I'm pretty good at complicated.'

'Get dressed,' I said. 'Meet us out front and we'll buy you a drink.'

'Give me ten,' he said.

I looked at Craig, still wriggling in Jerry's grasp.

'Don't worry about him,' Brewster said. 'I'll make sure he doesn't call the cops.'

I nodded to Jerry and said, 'Let him go.' I turned to Brewster. 'See you in ten.' I slammed Danny's locker closed and locked it.

Out front Jerry turned to me and said, 'Another cop?'

'I don't think this one is like Hargrove,' I said. 'Besides, he's with the sheriff's office.'

'Ain't he out of his jurisdiction?' Jerry asked.

'Probably,' I said, 'but what have we got to lose?'

SIXTY-THREE

Brewster came out, wearing a pair of jeans, a long-sleeved T-shirt, and loafers. He had on a brown windbreaker, I assumed to hide the gun he was wearing under his arm. He was also wearing a cream colored felt cowboy hat.

'There's a place around the corner,' he said. 'Danny and I get a drink there, sometimes, after we work out.'

'OK,' I said, 'lead the way.'

As we walked I said, 'This is Jerry.'

'How you doin'?' Brewster asked. 'I think Danny's mentioned you once or twice.'

'He has?'

'Nothing specific,' he promised.

Along the way he told us he was with the Sheriff's Department, but that he lived within the city limits. He and Danny only knew each other from the gym.

'I mean, I know he's a PI and he knows I'm a deputy, but we've never done business.'

'Until now,' I said.

'We'll see,' he said. 'If I can do something for him, maybe we'll just call it a favor.'

We stopped in front of a storefront.

'This is it?' I asked.

'This is it.'

Jerry and I both stared.

'It's a juice bar,' Jerry said, accusingly.

'I said we got drinks after we worked out,' he said. 'I didn't say it was liquor. Come on.'

Inside Brewster got a glass of carrot juice. Jerry and I tried to find something less offensive. He ended up with pineapple. I got apple. We took our drinks to a small plastic table. The seat creaked beneath Jerry's weight, but held.

'What's goin' on?' Brewster asked.

'Danny's been arrested for murder.'

'That's crazy. Danny's no killer.'

'Well, the cops say different.'

'Which cop?'

'Hargrove.'

'That prick?'

'I like you better already, Brewster,' I said.

'Me, too,' Jerry said.

'Tell me about it.'

'Before I do,' I said, 'you mind if I see your ID?'

'Of course not.'

He took out a leather folder which held his badge and ID. It said he was a detective with Clark County Sheriff's Department. I knew that the Sheriff's Department and the Las Vegas Police Department were not exactly a fraternity.

I handed it back, and told him the story.

'So it looks like your only lead is this guy Scaffazza,' he said. 'When is that gonna happen?'

'Soon, I hope.'

'Maybe there's something I can do,' Brewster said. 'I can talk to my boss, Ralph Lamb.'

Lamb had been the sheriff for two years at that point, on his way to making a big reputation for himself as a law and order guy.

'I don't think we want to get him involved at this point,' I said. 'It would pit him directly against the Las Vegas Police. That wouldn't be fair to him.'

'You're probably right.' He drank his carrot juice. 'Well, if there's anything else I can do, let me know.' He took out a business card and handed it to me. 'My home and work number are on there.'

I gave him my card, too.

'I ain't got a card,' Jerry told him.

Brewster grinned and said. 'That's OK. I wouldn't have one either, except the sheriff insists.'

I pushed my apple juice away. Jerry had actually finished his. We stood up, and the three of us walked out.

'Dwayne, let me ask you this,' I said. 'What are the chances somebody snuck into the locker room, got Danny's gun from his locker, killed Reynolds, and then returned the gun.'

'He'd have to be pretty quick,' Brewster said.

'Danny usually works out an hour, maybe an hour and a half. And he'd have to pick the lock, which wouldn't be hard on these lockers.'

'An hour and a half to drive to Reynolds' house, kill him, and drive back,' I said. 'Could be done. Was Danny at the gym the day of the murder?'

'I don't know,' Brewster said. 'I haven't been for a while. Today was actually my first day back.' He slapped his gut. 'Gotta work this off, again.'

'Well,' I said, 'I'll ask Danny.' I shook the deputy's hand. 'Thanks for your help up there.'

'Sure.' He said. 'Give Danny my best.' He reached past me to shake Jerry's hand.

'Who's Ralph Lamb?' Jerry asked.

'I'll explain on the way.'

'To where?'

'We have a show to go to.'

SIXTY-FOUR

Elvis' show was fantastic. He was the premier entertainer, not only with his singing and gyrating, but he had an endearing bond with his band, and with the audience. And he shocked everyone when he started singing 'Viva Las Vegas', and Ann-Margret came out from the wings to join him. With both talents on the stage, and their obvious chemistry, I was surprised it didn't just burst into flames.

At one point in the show Elvis took the time to point out and introduce Frank and Dino to the crowd. They both stood momentarily and graciously waved, and then saluted the young entertainer.

After the show Jerry and I were able to ride Frank and Dean's coat-tails and with no problem got backstage to see Elvis. Ann-Margret was gone by that time but there was still a crush of people back there trying to get to Elvis, comprised of friends, fans and press.

Since we were with Vegas royalty, we were ushered into Elvis' dressing room. He had already changed from his glittery stage suit into a robe, and had a towel around his neck. His black hair was wet and unruly.

'Kid,' Dean said, extending his hand, 'that was amazing.'

'Thank you, sir,' he said with his customary humility, 'comin' from you, that's a great compliment.'

'Yeah, Elvis,' Frank chimed in, 'you had the crowd in the palm of your hand – including us.'

They shook hands and Elvis said, 'I really appreciate that, sir.'

'Frank,' Frank said, 'just call me Frank.'

'Yes, sir.'

Elvis shook hands with me and Jerry, and when Frank and Dean said they had to go he asked us to stay behind.

'What's goin' on with the case?' he asked. I was surprised that he seemed more excited about that than his triumph on stage. Maybe he was just used to the adoration and success, but not to a murder investigation.

We told him what we'd been doing and he asked questions here and there. I didn't tell him about my meeting with Giancana. In fact, I hadn't even told Jerry.

'What made you look in the cereal boxes?' he asked Jerry.

'I knew a guy once who hid his drugs there,' Jerry said.

'And the freezer?' he asked me.

I shrugged and said, 'We'd looked everywhere else.'

'Sure wish I'd met that sheriff's deputy,' he said. 'He sounds like a good guy.'

'He is.'

'What about your friend, Danny?' he asked. 'Is he gettin' out on bail?'

'I talked with Kaminsky just before we came here,' I said. 'Danny walks out tomorrow morning. We'll be there to pick him up.'

'That's good,' he said. 'Mind if I tag along?'

'No, not at all,' I said, 'if you really want to.'

'I wanna meet your private eye buddy.'

'What about your boys?' I asked. 'And Red?'

'The boys are havin' a great time,' Elvis said. 'Red's a little pissed off, but I'll handle him. He just thinks it's his job to keep me safe.'

'Ain't it?' Jerry asked.

'It's not his job,' Elvis said, 'more like his ... calling, I guess.'

'He loves you,' I said.

'Yeah, he's my buddy,' Elvis said. 'I love him, too.'

'Bring him along,' Jerry said, and I looked at him, quickly.

I was relieved when Elvis said, 'Naw, that's OK. He can hang around the hotel and relax.'

'Well, OK,' I said. 'How about we pick you up tomorrow morning at eight?'

'In the back,' he said, as we all remembered the crowds in front of the hotel ever since his arrival.

'In the back,' I agreed.

'We'll have to make it quick, though,' Elvis

said. 'There's probably gonna be some fans and press there, too.'

'I'll just slow down,' Jerry said, 'and you can jump in.'

Elvis and I both looked at Jerry to see if he was actually joking.

'I could do that,' Elvis finally said.

'OK, we'll let you get some rest,' I said.

'You gonna be doin' anythin' tonight?' he asked. 'I don't wanna miss anymore good stuff.'

'You won't miss a thing,' I said. 'I'm goin' home and Jerry's goin' to his room.'

'I'll see you boys in the mornin', then.'

'Thanks for the tickets, Mr Presley,' Jerry said.

'My pleasure, son,' Elvis said.

Jerry and I left the room, made our way through the crowd until we were outside.

'Do I really gotta go to my room?' Jerry asked. 'I was kinda thinkin' I'd try some blackjack.'

'Pal,' I said, 'you can do anythin' you want.'

SIXTY-FIVE

When we got back to the Sands I stopped Jerry from getting out of the Caddy right away.

'I've got something to tell you.' He sat quiet while I relayed to him my late night visit with Sam Giancana. I wasn't sure whether or not he'd get mad I hadn't told him before, but there had never seemed to be time.

When I was done he asked, 'He really said that? "Don't kill 'im"?'

'Yes.'

'Why would he think you'd kill Scaffazza – or anyone? You ain't a killer, Mr G.'

'I know it,' I said. 'I was thinkin' the same thing.'

'I just realized Mr S. didn't say anythin' about a call from Johnny Roselli,' Jerry said. 'I wonder what's holdin' him up.'

'I don't know.'

'Look, Mr G.,' Jerry said, 'don't let what Mr Giancana said get to you. He just don't know who you really are.'

'Thanks, Jerry.'

'As far as Scaffazza goes,' Jerry said, 'I'll be

292

along with you, so don't worry, we'll find out what we wanna know.'

'Do you know him?' I asked. I didn't remember if I'd asked him that before.

'Never met 'im, never heard of 'im,' Jerry said. 'He's just another Giancana soldier, I guess.'

'Jerry,' I said, 'I don't want to kill Scaffazza – I mean, I don't want him killed.'

'I know that,' Jerry said. 'Don't worry, Mr G. I ain't plannin' on killin' him.'

'OK.'

'I don't kill easy, Mr G. I mean, it don't come easy to me.'

'I know it, Jerry.'

He nodded.

'You comin' in?' he asked.

'No, I'm goin' home to get some sleep. I didn't get much last night after Giancana's boys brought me back home.'

'Then I'll see ya in the mornin'.'

When I opened my front door the phone was ringing. I'm not one of those people who falls all over themselves trying to get to the phone before it can stop, but it could have had something to do with Danny's case, so I got to it before the third ring.

'Eddie? It's Frank.'

'Hey, Frank. Great show tonight, huh?'

'He called.'

'What?'

293

'Roselli,' Frank said. 'He called.'

'Are we set?'

'We are,' Frank said.

'Where?'

'A strip club called Star Shine.'

I knew the place. It was not a highly ranked strip club, as Vegas goes. But it was probably mob owned.

'When?'

'Tomorrow night – well, I guess it's tonight – at ten pm.'

'But where? In the parking lot? Behind the club? Inside?'

'I'm thinkin' inside,' Frank said. 'It's probably Scaffazza's idea, thinkin' he can't be whacked in a public place.'

'Why does everybody think I want to whack this guy? I don't whack people, Frank!'

'I know that, Eddie,' he said. 'Don't yell at me.'

'Sorry, sorry,' I said. 'Hey, I didn't tell you tonight that Danny's gettin' out tomorrow morning. We're gonna pick him up.'

'Good news,' he said. 'Who's we?'

'Me, Jerry and Elvis,' I said. 'The kid wants to come along.'

'That's fine,' Frank said. 'You can continue to keep him out of trouble, then. I mean, the kind of trouble the Colonel was thinking about.'

'I'm just hopin' he's not gonna want to come with us tomorrow night.'

'That's easy,' Frank said. 'Don't tell 'im.'

'Yeah, I guess.'

'OK,' Frank said, 'get some rest. You got a big day tomorrow.'

'Yeah, thanks. 'night. Frank.'

''night, Pally.'

I hung up. I had a big morning and a big night tomorrow. What was I going to do with the rest of the day?

SIXTY-SIX

I slept without interruption and awoke feeling good. After a shower I dressed casually and drove the Caddy to the Sands to pick up Jerry. He was wearing a sports jacket and already sweating as he got in on the passenger side.

'You heeled?' I asked.

He looked at me and said, 'Yeah.'

'Forty-five?'

He nodded. I knew he had somebody in Vegas who would leave a forty-five in a locker at the airport for him when he flew in. As far as I knew, though, he hadn't worn it up to now.

'Why now?' I asked, as I pulled out of the parking lot.

'I want to have it with me tonight,' he said, 'and I didn't know if we'd be getting back to the hotel between now and then. Don't worry, I'll put it in the glove compartment before we go to the police station.'

That didn't thrill me, either. There was no reason for the police to search my car, but if they did and found the gun, I'd go down for it.

When we got to the Riv the front was again

jammed with a mob of Elvis lovers. I wheeled around to the back, where there was a lesser, but no less enthusiastic, crowd.

I saw him come out the door with his 'Buzz' hat and shades. It fooled most of the crowd, but then somebody recognized him and pointed. Elvis sprinted for the car and it happened pretty much like Jerry said it would, only I was driving. I hadn't even come to a stop when Elvis vaulted into the back seat and shouted, 'Go, son, go!'

I hit the gas and peeled rubber in the parking lot, leaving behind a lot of disgruntled Elvis fans.

'Whoeee!' Elvis shouted, taking the hat and glasses off. 'That was somethin'.' He ran his hands through his hair.

'Yeah,' Jerry said, 'I'm all shook up.'

There was a moment of stunned silence, then we realized that, of course, Jerry was joking.

We all started to laugh.

By the time we pulled up in front of the police station Elvis had his hat and shades back on. I stopped the car and put the gear shift in park.

'Stay here, guys,' I said. 'Let's not crowd around the door.'

'OK, Mr G.'

Elvis sat back and waved his agreement.

I got out of the car and walked up to the front door. Kaminsky came out first, followed by Danny. The best you could say about him was that he looked as if he'd been run over by a car.

'I told you—' Kaminsky said to me, about to proudly proclaim himself a great lawyer, when there was a loud sound, and Danny went down. A blossom of red appearing in front of him.

It took me a moment to realize that Danny had been shot, and that blossom of red was an explosion of blood from his chest as the bullet hit him.

'Jesus Christ!' I yelled.

I could hear footsteps from behind me – undoubtedly Jerry and Elvis running up the side-walk. I stood stunned as police came pouring out the front door with guns drawn, some looking around for the shooter, others crowded around Danny. Somebody was on a radio, calling for an ambulance.

I didn't know if Danny was alive or dead.

SIXTY-SEVEN

Danny was alive.

They had an ambulance there in moments and whisked him off to the hospital. By the time we got there – Jerry driving because I was still stunned – Danny was already in the operating room.

The quick reactions of the police and the doctors saved his life.

My reaction didn't do anybody a damned bit of good, at all!

'All I did was stand there,' I said, as we sat in the waiting room.

'There wasn't nothin' else you could do, Mr G.,' Jerry said.

'Jerry's right, son,' Elvis said. 'What else could ya'll have done?'

'I could've helped him,' I said, 'that's what I could've done.'

'You're bein' too hard on yourself,' Jerry said.

'You gotta relax,' Elvis said. 'The good news is he's alive.'

'The bad news is I've got to tell Penny,' I

299

said.

'At least she wasn't there when it happened,' Jerry pointed out.

'Yeah, that's somethin', I guess.' I stood up. 'I guess I better call her.'

'Shouldn't you wait until you know more?' Elvis asked.

'No,' I said, 'as it is she's gonna be pissed at me for waitin' this long.'

'You want me to do it, Mr G.?' Jerry asked. 'In case the doctor comes out?'

'No, I have to do it,' I said. 'But come and get me if there's any need.'

'OK.'

I walked to the pay phones, dreading the call I had to make. As I expected she flipped out. I offered to have Jerry pick her up, but she said no, she'd get a cab and be right there.

I hung up, was about to head back to the waiting room when I decided to call Frank and Dean.

'You take it easy, pally,' Dean said. 'Let the doctors do their job and he should be fine.'

Frank said, 'Thank God he's alive, kid. I wonder if this has anythin' to do with Scaffazza bein' in town?'

'I don't know,' I said, 'but I'll find out tonight.'

Frank said he and Dean would probably stop at the hospital in a little while. I hung up thinking about Joey Scaffazza. I'd been so pissed at people thinking I wanted to kill him. I was now convinced that if I found out he was involved in shooting Danny, I *would* kill him in a minute.

When Penny arrived she was like a rock. Instead of dissolving into tears in my arms as I had expected, she punched me in the stomach in front of Jerry and Elvis. Penny hits hard.

'How dare you not call me right away, Eddie Gianelli!' she said.

'Penny ... I...'

She took my face in her hands and said, 'I know ... how is he?'

'Alive,' I said. 'They're still working on him.'

'How bad?'

'He was shot once in the chest, near the heart.'

'Oh, no problem, then,' she said.

'What?'

She put her hand over my heart and said, 'Danny's got a heart of stone. We both know that.'

By the time the doctor came out Frank Sinatra and Dean Martin were there, and Elvis had taken off the hat and shades. The doctor, a smooth-faced young man in his thirties, did a double take.

'Who ... is there family here?'

Penny pushed me forward.

'I'm afraid I'm the closest thing to family,

doc,' I said.

'I mean real family,' the doctor said, 'blood relatives?'

'There are none,' I said. 'His family has all passed. You're gonna have to settle for me, doc. Danny and I grew up together.'

He studied me, then the other people in the waiting room. There were a couple of new fathers there who had forgotten about their babies when they saw Frank, Dean and Elvis.

'And the rest?' he asked.

'Friends,' I said, 'all friends.'

'Come on, doc,' Frank said. 'Be a pal.'

The doctor had removed his surgical hat but still had the mask around his neck. He pulled that off now and said, 'Oh, all right. It was touch and go for a while. The bullet nicked the left ventricle. We didn't see the damage at first, but once we did we repaired it. Removing it did some other damage which is simply going to hurt like hell while it's healing. The bullet went in, and did not come out, so we removed it. He's going to hurt from that for a while, too.'

'But he will heal?' Penny asked.

'Yes, ma'am,' the doctor said. 'He'll heal. It will take a while, but he'll heal. As long as nobody shoots him again.' He looked at me. 'My name is Dr Markinson. We'll talk again.'

He put his hand out and I shook it. He had a good grip, held on when I tried to let go.

'I'm going to want show tickets,' he said.

'No problem, doc,' I said, pumping his hand.

'Any show you want.'

Markinson nodded, released my hand, turned and walked away.

I turned to Penny. This time she did collapse into my arms.

SIXTY-EIGHT

We all sat around a while longer. Dr Markinson came out again and said that Danny wouldn't wake up until morning.

'Can we go in for a minute?' Penny asked him. 'Just to see him?'

Markinson looked at me.

'She just wants to see him breathing.'

'Sure,' he said, 'for a minute – but just the two of you.'

I turned to the others. 'You guys should get goin'. I really appreciate you being here.'

'I'll stay,' Frank said. 'We got an appointment soon, Eddie.'

I looked at my watch. I hadn't realized that we'd been there all day, and it was nine p.m. We were supposed to meet with Scaffazza at ten.

'Right.'

'Me and Jerry will stay, too,' Elvis said.

'Well, I gotta get back to the hotel,' Dean said. 'I'm supposed to call Jeannie.' He looked at Frank. 'I'll take the limo.'

'No problem, Dag,' Frank said. 'Dag' was

Frank's nickname for Dino. It was short for Dago.

'Eddie...' Penny said, grabbing my arm.

'OK, let's go.'

The doctor took us into the room where Danny was laid out, hooked up to beeping, blinking machines.

'Two minutes,' he said, and left.

Danny was pale and seemed shrunken. But the important thing was, he was breathing, his chest rising and falling steadily.

Penny moved close to the bed and put her hand on his chest.

'We're here, Danny,' she said. 'Eddie and I are here. And I'll be here until you wake up.'

She leaned over and kissed his cheek, then looked at me. I don't know if she wanted me to say something to him, but instead I said, 'We better go.'

She nodded, and we left the room. Before we got to the waiting room she asked, 'What's this appointment you have tonight? Does it have to do with what happened to Danny?'

'It has to do with you, Danny, and Billy Reynolds,' I said. 'And yeah, it may have to do with Danny being shot.'

'Then go and keep your appointment, Eddie,' she said. 'I'll be here when Danny wakes up.'

'Are you sure' I asked. 'The doctor said he might sleep til morning.'

'That's OK,' she said. 'I'll be here.'

'OK,' I said. 'I'll be back. Jerry and me, we'll

be back. And we'll bring you some food.'

'I'm not hungry.'

'Maybe not now,' I said, 'but trust me, you will be.'

When we got to the waiting room I said, 'OK, guys, let's go.'

I couldn't remember if Frank and Penny had ever met before, but he went to her and gave her an encouraging hug. Then Elvis did the same thing. Finally, even Jerry hugged her.

I went over and gave her a kiss on the cheek.

'See you later.'

She grabbed a handful of my shirt and said, 'Be careful.'

'We will.'

We all left the waiting room, and the hospital.

SIXTY-NINE

The better strip clubs in Vegas are usually located on Las Vegas Blvd. 'Better' means 'classier'. Want something dirtier and cheaper? That would take you to Industrial Road. The Star Shine looked to be on the lower edge of the scale as we pulled into the parking lot with Jerry at the wheel. There were about half a dozen cars in the lot. None of them would belong to the strippers, or other employees. Traditionally, they parked in the back.

'How do you wanna play this?' Frank asked.

'I think Jerry should go in first, get himself seated,' I said. 'Then you and I can go in and look for Scaffazza.'

'What about me?' Elvis demanded.

'You're gonna stay out here.'

'No I ain't, either,' he said, sounding like the little boy he must've been in Tupelo. 'I came along to see some action.'

'This isn't the kind of action the Colonel wants you around, Elvis,' I said.

'Frank's goin' in,' he said.

'Frank set up the meeting,' I said. 'Scaffazza's probably going to expect Frank. Besides, that's the way we'll recognize each other. I don't know Scaffazza and he doesn't know me, but he knows what Frank looks like.'

'Do you think he knows Jerry?' Frank asked.

'I don't know the guy,' Jerry said.

'Yeah, but maybe he's seen you before,' Frank said. 'You've been in LA a time or two.'

'I think we'll have to take the chance,' I said.

'I'm goin' in, Eddie,' Elvis insisted. 'I'll keep on the hat and glasses. But if you try to leave me in the car, I'll just follow you in.'

I looked at Jerry and Frank and they both just shrugged.

'OK,' I said, 'you go in after Jerry. Don't sit near him, though. And don't get any lap dances. A girl in your lap is sure to recognize you.'

'OK, boss,' he said. 'Now, how about a gun?'

'Elvis,' I said, 'you don't have a gun on you, do you?'

'No,' he said, 'that's why I'm askin' for one.'

'No guns,' I said. 'Jerry's got a gun. That should be enough if something goes ... wrong.'

'If somethin' does go wrong, Mr Presley,' Jerry said, 'just hit the floor.'

'Jerry,' Elvis said, 'why don't ya'all just call me Elvis?'

'Forget it,' I said. 'In all these years I can't even get him to call me Eddie.'

Jerry went in first. We waited a few minutes

and then I said, 'OK, Elvis, go ahead. Remember what I said.'

'Right,' Elvis said, 'stay away from Jerry, and don't get any lap dances.'

'Right,' I said, 'go.'

Frank and I sat in the Caddy and watched Elvis go inside.

'If this goes sideways...' I said.

'...the Colonel will have both of our asses.'

'Let's wait about ten minutes,' I said, looking at my watch. It was nine fifty-five.

'Frank, is there going to be anyone else with Scaffazza? One of Roselli's guys?'

'I don't know,' Frank said. 'Johnny did say he'd have Scaffazza delivered.'

'I guess we'll have to wait and see.'

At ten-oh-five I said, 'OK, let's go.'

We got out of the car and walked to the door. We were almost to it when I remembered something Frank liked to do. Something I should have asked him already.

'Frank,' I said, 'you don't have a gun on you, do you?'

'You bet I do, pally.'

Suddenly, I wished I had one, too.

SEVENTY

Jerry told me later that as soon as he entered the club he knew something was wrong.

'It's just a feelin' you get, Mr G.,' he said, 'but you learn to trust it after so many years.'

He looked around, saw several of the tables with one or two men seated at them. There was also a table with about five men, who seemed to be there for some kind of party, maybe a bachelor party. He decided to get a table away from them. He managed to isolate himself toward the back of the room, and waved off two girls who headed straight for him. He did, however, order a $7.00 beer from a waitress.

'Seven dollars, Mr G.!'

Luckily, he managed to refocus after that shock.

Elvis walked in, spotted Jerry and simply took a table as far from the big guy as he could. This put him in close proximity to the bachelor party. He also ordered a $7.00 beer, but from a different waitress, and without complaint.

Frank and I walked in, stopped just inside the door and looked around. There was no way to pick out Joey Scaffazza. However, a man who was sitting with another man stood up and approached us. He was not dressed like a hood – like the two guys who had taken me to Sam Giancana. He was dressed casually with a T-shirt and slacks. If he had a gun on him, I couldn't see it.

'Mr Sinatra?'

'Yeah,' Frank said.

The guy looked at me.

'Eddie Gianelli.'

He nodded and said, 'Oh, right.' He looked back at Frank. 'Mr Roselli said I was to deliver Joey Scaffazza to you. There he is.'

Scaffazza was a nervous looking guy in his thirties, also dressed casually so he couldn't hide a gun.

'I'll be over here,' the guy said, and walked away. He seated himself at an empty table near Jerry, who eyed the guy critically.

Frank and I walked over to Scaffazza.

'Joey?' Frank asked.

'Yeah, that's right.' Scaffazza wasn't only nervous, he was downright jumpy.

'This is Eddie Gianelli,' Frank said. 'He wants to talk to you.'

'So talk,' Scaffazza said. His sunken eyes had deep shadows beneath them. I didn't know if this was natural, or from lack of sleep.

We sat. The bachelor party guys were making a racket with two of the girls who had stopped by their table.

'I had a talk with Sam Giancana the other night,' I said.

'Yeah?'

'He told me to be sure not to kill you.'

'That was nice of Sam.'

'Yeah,' I said, 'but that was before a friend of mine was shot. If I find out you had anything to do with that—'

'I didn't have nothin' to do with nobody gettin' shot,' Scaffazza said. 'I told that to Mr Roselli.'

'You're here because I wanted to talk to you about Billy Reynolds. The other shooting happened just this morning.'

'I wasn't even here this mornin',' Scaffazza said. 'We just got in from LA a couple of hours ago.' He jerked his chin. 'You can check with that mook.'

'I will,' I said. 'Tell me about Reynolds.'

He frowned and bit the inside of his cheek, then went to work on a non-existent thumbnail.

'Come on, Joey,' Frank said. 'Don't make me have to tell Johnny you weren't cooperative.' Then he added, 'Or Momo.'

'Look, Mr Sinatra,' Joey said. 'I know you're good friends with Mr Giancana. Can you get me to Chicago ... alive?'

'Probably,' Frank said. 'Depends on how co-operative you are.'

'I'm sure that *stronzo* over there has orders to kill me,' Joey said. 'I ain't never gettin' back to LA alive.'

'We'll get you to Chicago,' I said. 'But you have to talk to me.'

Scaffazza scratched an armpit and asked, 'Whataya wanna know?'

'Who killed Billy Reynolds?'

'I don't know,' he said, 'but I can guess.'

'So guess.'

'Johnny.'

'You're sayin' Roselli came here and killed him?' I asked.

'Naw, naw, but he had him killed.'

'By who?'

'Again, I'm guessin' here.'

'Go ahead.'

'Frankie Bonpensiero.'

'And who's he?' I asked.

'One of Johnny's top button men.'

'Why would he send Bonpensiero here to kill Reynolds?' I asked.

'Reynolds was doin' business on Johnny's turf,' Scaffazza said. 'Worse, he was makin' money, which means he was takin' money from Johnny.'

'That's worth killin' over,' Frank said.

'Where's Bonpensiero now?' I asked.

'Who knows?' Scaffazza asked. 'Probably back in LA. And if it wasn't him it was one of Johnny's other guys. So what I'm sayin' is Johnny killed your guy.'

I looked at Frank. 'Why try to pin it on Danny? When the mob orders a hit isn't it supposed to send a message?'

313

'There ain't so many hits bein' done, any-more,' Scaffazza said. 'The button guy – Bon-pensiero, or whoever – probably wanted it to look like somethin' else.'

'A crime of passion,' Frank said. 'Maybe he just took advantage of the fact that Reynolds was Penny's old boyfriend, and Penny worked for Danny.'

I looked at Scaffazza. 'Why should I believe you?'

'Hey,' Scaffazza said, 'I could lie to you, but why should I? You're gonna keep me alive long enough to get to Chicago, right?'

'Right,' Frank said, 'if we believe you.'

'Were you workin' with Reynolds?'

Scaffazza hesitated, then said, 'Well, yeah, I was.'

'Then why didn't Roselli have you killed?'

'Politics.'

'What do you mean, politics? What kinda politics?' I asked.

'I think Johnny knew all along that I was workin' for Mr Giancana,' Scaffazza said. 'So he fired me, but didn't have me killed.'

'But he killed Reynolds.'

'Reynolds wasn't in the family,' Scaffazza said. 'He had to be killed.'

'Then what makes you think you're gonna be killed here, in Vegas?' I asked.

'Because it's Vegas,' Scaffazza said. 'Any-thin' can happen in Vegas, right? Even though Johnny runs Vegas for the mob, he can claim I

314

got killed over a girl, or a gambling debt.' He gnawed on his thumb. 'Or maybe I'm wrong and he's not gonna have me killed. But I don't wanna take the chance.'

I sat back in my chair and looked at Frank. 'What do you think?'

'It makes sense to me,' Frank said, 'as much as this crazy mob shit can make sense.'

'OK,' I said, 'so Reynolds was hit by the mob. They tried to pin it on Danny. How do I prove that? They still insist it was Danny's gun.'

Frank shrugged.

'What's Bonpensiero look like?' I asked.

'Tall, dark-haired,' Scaffazza said. 'He's got these powerful lookin' shoulders and chest, but he carries a gut with him.'

That rang a bell. Why?

'Who else was Reynolds workin' with?' I asked.

'He had a crew.'

'What about them?' I asked. 'Where are they?'

'I don't know,' Scaffazza said. 'I wouldn't know them if they was sittin' at the next table.'

For some reason that made me look over at the bachelor party just as the five guys produced guns and stood up, upsetting their table.

'Down!' I shouted.

SEVENTY-ONE

I pushed Frank down and upset our own table. Scaffazza had already moved.

Elvis had been sitting right near the five party guys. He stood up now, picked up a chair and threw it at them. At the same time Jerry got up and pulled his forty-five. Roselli's delivery boy produced a gun from somewhere – ankle holster? – and he and Jerry started shooting. The girls started screaming and running for cover, as did the other customers.

From the floor, Frank pulled out his gun – a silver .38 – and started firing.

A couple of the bachelor party guys got off some shots, the others had ducked the chair Elvis threw. It cost them.

Jerry was deadly with his gun, I'd seen him do it before, and he rarely missed. Plus he'd been ready for trouble, because he'd had a bad feeling from the moment he walked in.

Elvis did some more chair work, picking up another one and this time slamming it over somebody's head. I was wishing he had just plastered himself to the floor.

I heard a couple of bullets hit our overturned table. Frank returned fire. Jerry and Roselli's man kept firing, and then suddenly it was quiet.

I lifted my head up for a look.

The place had emptied out of customers and girls. The only people I saw standing were Jerry and Roselli's guy. Elvis had finally hit the floor.

'Looks like it's over,' Frank said, standing up.

I was afraid Scaffazza was dead, figuring he was the main target, but he was sitting up with his hand clasped to his arm, blood streaming from between his fingers. Not unscathed, but not dead.

'Mr G.?'

I turned, saw Jerry standing next to me.

'You OK?' he asked.

I looked down at myself, took stock, and said, 'Yeah, I seem to be. Elvis?'

The King stood up and waved. 'I'm OK.'

I turned and looked at Roselli's guy.

'You OK?'

'Yeah'

He walked over to the bachelor party, checked out the bodies.

'They're all dead.'

'Frank?'

'I'm OK.'

I righted our table, and a chair, and helped Scaffazza into it.

'What the fuck!' he said.

'Those guys must have been Reynolds' crew,' I said. I couldn't figure it any other way.

'Amateurs,' Roselli's guy said, 'so you're probably right'

'What's your name?' I asked him.

'Sal.'

'Sal's got a point,' Jerry said. 'They never should have sat together, shouldn't have been makin' that much noise.'

'Did you guys drive here?' I asked Sal.

'Yeah, we did.'

'They must've followed you,' I said, 'figured to kill Joey in Vegas – and you.'

'Scumbags,' Sal said. 'You're right, they never would've tried this in LA. Johnny would've had their nuts.'

'OK,' I said, 'everybody out.'

'What?' Jerry said.

'You've got to scram out of here before the cops get here.'

'What about you?' Jerry asked.

'I'm gonna stay,' I said. 'I'm gonna try to pin Reynolds' death on these guys. Or at least prove that it could have been somebody other than Danny. For that I need to stay.'

'I'm stayin', too,' Frank said.

'Frank—'

'I'm sure somebody recognized me,' he said. 'The cops would come lookin' for me, anyway. I might as well face the music, now.'

'OK,' I said, 'but give your gun to Jerry.'

'Good idea.' He handed it over.

'Mr G.—'

'If you stay, Jerry, they're gonna toss your ass in a cell because of your gun – and maybe for killin' some of these guys. You, too, Sal. Get out.'

'Who you gonna say killed them?' Sal asked.

'I don't know,' I said. 'Me and Frank were sittin' here having a drink with our buddy Joey when suddenly two sets of guys started shooting. These guys ended up dead, and the other ones took off.'

Sal thought it over and said, 'That could work.'

'It better work,' I said. 'Now get out. I think I hear sirens.'

'What about me?' Scaffazza asked.

'You're goin' to the hospital,' I said, 'and after that, Chicago.'

'What if they lock my ass up?'

'I've got a good Jewish lawyer for you.'

SEVENTY-TWO

The first car to respond brought two uniformed cops, one of whom was impressed with Frank. The second vehicle to arrive was an ambulance, with two attendants, one of whom was impressed with Frank.

All the customers were gone, and the girls had gone home, so there were no witnesses. The club manager talked to the two cops, saying he wasn't sure which girls were on and which were off. It was going to take a while to put together the facts of who was there, let alone who saw what. It would fall to the detectives.

When the detectives arrived I was pleased to see that it was not Hargrove and his partner, Martin. However, that feeling didn't last for long. About fifteen minutes later, while Frank and I were being questioned and Scaffazza was being bandaged, Hargrove walked in with Martin trailing behind.

'Well, well,' he said. 'I knew when I heard Sinatra's name I was going to find you here, Eddie.' He looked around. 'Come on, bullets flying all around? Where's the big guy?'

'Who?'

'Epstein.'

'Jerry wasn't here.'

He pointed his finger at me.

'If I find out you're lying—'

'How are you gonna find that out?' I asked, cutting him off. 'You don't even have any witnesses.'

Hargrove looked at the other detectives for confirmation. They just nodded and shrugged.

'Don't go away,' he said to me and Frank. He grabbed one of the responding detectives by the arm and pulled him aside.

'Wanna tell me what happened while my partner's distracted?' Martin asked.

'Frank, Joey and me—'

'Joey?'

'Oh, this is our friend, Joey Scaffazza. Joey took a stray bullet.'

'Uh-huh,' Martin said, 'a stray bullet.' He folded his arms. 'Keep going.'

I told him the story of being caught in the crossfire between two apparently warring factions.

Martin looked around, then turned back at me.

'I can't wait to tell Hargrove this story,' he said, finally. 'Wait here.'

'These guys got it out for you?' Scaffazza asked.

'One of them does, yeah.'

'Not much changes city to city, huh?'

'Nope, not much.'

'They're gonna find out I'm from LA.'

'There are a lot of people in Vegas from LA,' I said. 'Doesn't mean a thing. Just stick to the story.'

'Ya know, you're a stand-up guy,' Scaffazza said.

'As long as you had nothing to do with shooting my friend, you'll be fine.'

'I swear. Ask Sal. We wasn't even here.'

'Well, just sit back and relax,' I said. 'We're gonna be here a while.'

I knew Frank could make a phone call and leave. It was to his credit that he stuck it out with Scaffazza and me. We spent two hours there, and another three at the police station. Hargrove had us taken to his building, claiming the case was an extension of his murder investigation. Since it was going to take forever to collect the witnesses the other detectives did not argue.

They separated us to see if our stories would hold up.

Hargrove walked into the interrogation room and sat down across from me.

'You wanna make a phone call, Eddie?' he asked. 'Maybe to your buddy Robert Kennedy?'

'We're not buddies,' I said. 'Am I under arrest?'

'Not at all.'

'Then I don't need a phone call, do I?'

He questioned me for half an hour, trying to poke holes in my story. I denied, denied, denied any knowledge of what had happened in that club. I didn't know if the cops were going to be able to collect any witnesses. Certainly they wouldn't be able to reassemble the customers who were there. I would have been surprised if one of those guys didn't have a record. It was that kind of club. And the same went for the girls who worked there. There'd be no love lost between them and the cops. If they came up with one witness who would describe Jerry, or 'Buzz,' or Sal it would be a miracle.

I stuck to my guns.

But in the end I called Kaminsky and he got us out. It was just taking too long. Oh, we all stuck to our stories. Or so I thought.

Kaminsky came in and said, 'Come on, you and Frank are out.'

'Me and Frank? What about Scaffazza?'

'Your LA mafia buddy talked.'

'What do you mean he talked?' I asked.

'Come on, bubula,' Kaminsky said, 'Kaminsky wants to get out of here.'

'Yeah, well, Eddie G. wants an explanation.' I sat back down and folded my arms.

'He confessed.'

'To what?'

'To working with Reynolds on Roselli's turf.'

'So he's under arrest?'

'No,' Kaminsky said, 'he's in protective custody. Our other buddy Hargrove is going to try to use him to take down Roselli.'

'What?' I said. 'Roselli's big time. Hargrove is *not* big time.'

'I know it and you know it. Hargrove, he don't know it. Anyway, they're dropping the charges against Danny. They now feel sure Reynolds' murder was a mafia hit, and Danny was the fall guy.'

'What?' I was amazed. 'How did they—'

'What does it matter how?' Kaminsky asked. 'Danny's my client, you're my client, for to-night even the Chairman of the Board is my client, and I got you all off.'

'I want to talk to Joey.'

'What, you made friends with this *schlimazel* in one night?'

'We bonded over beer and boobs,' I said. 'I want to talk to him.'

Kaminsky stared at me, frustrated, then said, 'Wait.' He shook his head, muttered, *'Putz,'* and went out.

SEVENTY-THREE

I was given five minutes with Scaffazza. He was sitting in an interview room, his hands folded on the table in front of him, looking as calm as could be.

'What are you doing?' I asked, even before I sat across from him.

'It's better this way,' he said. 'I'm safer in custody than I'd be in LA or Chicago. Or even here in Vegas.'

'Who do you think is gonna come after you?' I asked. 'If that was Reynolds' crew, they're all dead.'

'Maybe,' he said, 'but I can't trust Johnny, either. I think Sal was gonna kill me. Besides, this'll help you.'

'Me? Why do you want to help me?'

'You put your life on the line for your buddy,' he said. 'You stayed behind to take the heat in that club when you didn't have to. And you didn't throw me to the wolves. I told you, you're a stand-up guy. This'll get you and your buddy off the hook.'

'For now, maybe,' I said, 'but Hargrove will

keep coming.'

'Well,' Scaffazza said, 'maybe this will get him off your back for a while. It's the least I can do. You guys were gonna help me.'

'Joey—'

'Hey, listen,' he said, 'this satisfies me. It should satisfy you. They droppin' the charges against your friend?'

'Yes.'

'Good.'

'But I'm still wondering about his gun,' I said. 'If the police are convinced his gun killed Reynolds, why would they let him go?'

'Maybe,' Scaffazza said, 'they faked that part of the evidence.'

'You mean ... they lied?'

Scaffazza shrugged. 'They're cops, ain't they?'

'But ... you're trusting them.'

He shrugged. 'Ya gotta trust somebody some time. As long as I can give them information about Roselli, they'll keep me alive.'

'What about Giancana?'

'I won't tell them anything about Giancana,' Scaffazza said, 'Just Roselli.'

I stared at him for a few moments. He did look very satisfied with himself.

'OK, Joey,' I said, 'have it your way. Thanks.'

'That's OK,' he said. 'Maybe I'll come back to town some time. You can show me around.'

'I'll do that,' I said. 'You can bet on it.'

I knocked on the door to be let out.

* * *

Frank went back to the Sands. He'd had enough for one night.

'I need one more favor,' I told him.

'What is it?'

'I need somebody in Chicago checked out. Do you know anyone?'

'I got just the guy,' he said. 'Gimme your guy's info.'

I wrote it out for him. We drove to the hospital, but he had a limo pick him up out front.

Kaminsky and I went inside. Penny was sitting in the waiting room. When she saw us she got to her feet.

'How is he?' I asked.

'Still asleep. What time is it?'

I looked at my watch.

'Six a.m. I was supposed to bring you some food, but ... things happened.'

'It's OK.'

'I'll get us all some breakfast,' Kaminsky said. 'Be right back.'

I nodded, sat down with Penny.

'How did your meeting go?' she asked.

'Fine,' I said. 'Danny's off the hook for the murder. They're dropping all charges.'

'What? How? Why?'

'They're goin' after somethin' bigger,' I said.

'Well ... that's wonderful.'

'But I'm still confused about his gun,' I said. 'Unless Hargrove lied – and he's a lot of things, but not a liar – then how do they have

327

Danny's gun pegged as the murder weapon?'

'And if they still do, why drop the charges? Eddie, maybe they were lying.'

'I keep thinkin' about Danny's gym.'

'His gym?'

'We checked his locker,' I said. 'That's what the extra key was for.'

'What did you find?' she asked.

'Just what you'd expect to find in a locker at a gym,' I said. 'Nothing else. But what if he left his gun in his locker while he worked out and somebody took it?'

'He doesn't usually do that.'

'But what if he did it that day? Somebody could have taken it out, killed Billy, and put it back.'

'Who?' she asked. 'Do you know who did kill Billy?'

'Not exactly,' I said, 'but it could have been a hit man sent by Johnny Roselli.'

'Why would he want to frame Danny?'

'So nobody would think it was a hit.'

'I don't know if Danny went to the gym that day.'

'I'll ask him,' I said, 'some time. You know, we talked to this deputy sheriff who works out with Danny—'

'What? Who?'

'A deputy sheriff named Brewster, Dwayne Brewster. He has the locker next to Danny's.'

'Eddie,' she said, 'Danny doesn't know any

deputy named Brewster.'

'We met him,' I said. 'He said he worked out with Danny. Even took us to a juice bar where they sometimes get a drink afterwards.'

'Do you hear what you're saying?' she asked. 'Danny in a juice bar?'

She was right. The idea was ludicrous.

'I checked his ID.'

'They can be faked,' she said.

And then it hit me. Scaffazza's description of Roselli's hit man, Bonpensiero. It matched Brewster perfectly, right down to the gut.

'Damn,' I said. We'd been talking to the guy who probably killed Reynolds. The guy who probably took the gun from Danny's locker and used it.

The guy who tried to get me to drink apple juice.

'What is it?'

'Never mind,' I said. Bonpensiero was probably already back in LA. His job was done. 'It's all over now, anyway. Danny's off the hook, and that's all we wanted, right?'

'Right,' she said, 'well, that and Danny alive.'

I had told Brewster that Danny was getting out of jail in the morning. He probably figured if he took Danny out, he'd die with the blame for Reynolds' murder still on him.

There was no way I was going to LA to hunt down a hired killer. Bonpensiero was out of my league. Besides, Roselli would probably have him looking for Scaffazza now, and leave Danny alone.

I'd have to be satisfied with what Penny said. Danny was off the hook, and alive.

EPILOGUE

'What happened with Elvis?' Roger Bennett asked.

'He went back to Memphis,' I said.

'Did you see him again? Did you stay friends?'

'I saw him when he came back to Vegas in '67 to marry Priscilla. And then again in '69 when the International opened. That's when he really hit it big in Las Vegas.'

'So you didn't stay friends?'

'We were friends, Roger,' I said, 'but I wasn't part of the Memphis Mafia. We weren't that close.'

Roger and I were in a small restaurant just down the street from our building. It wasn't a place I'd take a lady friend for dinner, but it was certainly good enough for lunch.

'Hey, I got a question,' Roger said.

'I thought you'd have a lot.'

'When Elvis hit that guy over the head with that chair, did he kill 'im?'

'You know, he asked me the same thing later,' I said. 'It really bothered him. Fact is, all those guys were killed by bullets. Elvis just helped him hit the floor.'

I sipped my coffee, knowing I was going to pay for it later. I usually had a cup in the morning, and another in the evening. Another by-product of being in my eighties. Coffee was not my friend.

'What about the plate number?'

'That turned out to be Danny's car, after all. The woman got the plate right, she just wasn't sure when she saw it.'

'But what about Danny's shooting?' Roger asked. 'Did you ever find out the truth about that? Was it Bon ... Bon ... what's his name? The hit man?'

'As a matter of fact,' I said, 'it wasn't...'

A couple of days after Elvis had gone back to Memphis, and both Frank and Dean had left town, I got two phone calls. The first was from Frank, calling me from Palm Springs.

'Hey, Frank, you back in town?'

'Naw, I'm home. I just wanted to tell you I heard from my guy in Chicago.'

'Oh, OK.' I'd forgotten I'd asked him to check on Albert Kroner for me. From his hospital bed Danny had told me to stop worrying about Kroner. He'd take care of that case when he got back on his feet. So I did it. I forgot.

'What'd you find out?'

He told me...

* * *

Later that day I got a call at the Sands from Connie, the bartender in Laughlin.

'Hey, Mr Gianelli? It's Connie. From the Riverside?'

'Oh, hi, Connie,' I said. I asked him the same thing I'd asked Frank. 'You in town?' Figuring he was coming over for a job interview.

'Naw, I'm still in Laughlin. But you asked me to watch our handy man, Ed Rosette?'

'Yeah?'

'Strangest thing,' Connie said. 'I followed him one day—'

'You what?'

'I followed him.'

'Connie, I just meant for you to keep an eye on him.'

'Well, I did, I followed him. And listen to this. He goes to this empty lot and starts shooting this rifle.'

'A rifle?'

'Yeah, a fancy one with a scope? Kinda weird, huh?' he asked.

'Yeah, weird.'

'That's what I figured, so I followed him again, did it for a couple of days. And he does the same thing, only get this. Every day he gets better. On the third day, he's hittin' his targets – buncha tin cans – every time. Can you imagine a guy gettin' that good at somethin' in that short a time?'

'That is strange, Connie,' I said. 'Listen, thanks.'

'Yeah, sure,' Connie said. 'I, uh, still intend to come to Vegas to apply for that job.'

'You do that,' I said, 'and I'll make sure you get it.'

Elvis, Frank and Dino might have left town, but Jerry decided to stay for a while. He played the ponies. I found him at the Sands sports book and asked, 'Wanna take a ride?'

'Where?'

'Laughlin.'

'Hey, that's the place you took Elvis for that ninety-eight cent chicken dinner.'

'That's the place.'

'Let's go.'

I figured the best way to brace Rosette was at work. He wouldn't expect it.

He was around the side of the motel, this time, but still using the hose.

'Hey, Rosette!' I called.

He looked up, saw me standing there, and straightened. He also saw Jerry standing behind me.

'Whataya want?'

'I want you to drop the act, Albert,' I said.

'What? What did you call me?'

'I called you by your real name. Albert Kroner. A Chicago lawyer who embezzled two million dollars from his clients.'

He laughed. 'I look like I got two million bucks?'

'You look exactly like a guy who has two million dollars, but doesn't want anyone to know about it. You also have a job that a guy with a genius IQ, who can learn to do anything in a few days, would have.'

'I don't know what you're talkin' about.'

'We talked to some of your neighbors in Chicago, Albert,' I said. 'They didn't like you much, said you weren't very friendly. But you know what they each said? You were remarkable. You could teach yourself to do anything in a very short time. One guy said – and get this – that if you ever got disbarred, you'd make a great handy man.'

He dropped the hose, wiped his hands on his pants. He looked around, maybe for a weapon. I doubt he had the rifle anywhere near the hotel. Maybe in his car.

'After the last time I was here you decided you needed to learn how to shoot, so you bought yourself an expensive rifle – maybe a sniper's rifle – and you started practicing. Then you came to Vegas and waited for your chance to shoot Danny Bardini. Probably followed me – and you could've taught yourself how to do that without being spotted.'

He didn't say anything.

'I got a question, Albert,' I said. 'How come a genius like you didn't think to shoot me?'

He stared at me, licked his lips, then said, 'I figured you worked for Bardini, and if I got rid of him, that would be the end of it.' Suddenly, his speech pattern was more like a lawyer than like a handy man. 'So what now, Mr Gianelli?'

'Now,' I said, 'you go back to Chicago to give those people their money back.'

'And if I don't?'

'My buddy Jerry, here, will break your back.'

'It appears you leave me no choice.'

'Jerry,' I said.

Jerry took a step back and waved. Two uniformed police officers appeared and approached Albert Kroner.

'Go with these nice men, Albert,' I said. 'They'll arrange for you to be extradited to Illinois.'

As the two police officers marched Kroner to their car, Jerry asked, 'Can we get that ninety-eight cent chicken dinner now?'

'Wow,' Roger said, regarding me across the table. He wasn't dressed like Elvis, but he still had the hair and sideburns. It was almost like sitting across from the King. If I put a hat and glasses on him. 'I guess they were right about you, Mr G.'

'What do you mean?'

'You really did have everything it took to be a good private eye.'